Triumphant Empire

Dodge Merrin

Paperback ISBN-13: 979-8-9909079-2-8

Cover design by Calley Dunnihoo

Content Warning: *This book contains depictions of science fiction themed violence.*

Contents

Prologue: Shattered

Vehla
United
Wednesday, January 23rd, 2707
10:02 A.M.

"What are you doing?" Chancellor Macey shouted as several protection agents burst into his office.

"We're taking you to the fortress. An Ordonian fleet has entered the system, and they outnumber us three-to-one," the lead agent, Hain, responded. Two others grabbed the chancellor and practically dragged him from the office.

"How did they get so close, and why don't we have more ships here in the home system?" Macey asked, his earlier anger giving way to flustered confusion. He tried to get his feet under him, but the agents easily held up his lean frame and moved faster than he could keep up.

"They've destroyed a large portion of our nationwide sensor net and many of our ships were sent out to defend elsewhere. General Reno expected the surrounding systems to be attacked first."

"Where is the general now?"

"Already at the fortress, sir."

"I want to talk to him."

"He's busy coordinating the defense, and we need to get you to safety. You can talk to him once we reach the fortress."

They reached the chancellery's garage level where a convoy of six vehicles was already waiting: two limousines and four agency SUV's. The chancellor and agents piled into one of the limos, then the convoy immediately sped away.

"Are the defenses holding?" Macey questioned.

"No. The enemy is aggressively pushing toward the homeworld, ignoring all our other holdings in the system."

The chancellor looked through a side window and towards the sky where he was able to see several bursts of light from weapons fire which showed clearly in the dark sky created by Vehla's blue sun.

They exited the city, and he looked back to watch it recede into the distance as they pulled away at high speed, the road having already been cleared ahead of them.

"Get down!" Hain shouted as he grabbed the chancellor and pushed him to the floor then threw himself on top just as the car was hit by a massive force and sent spinning through the air.

It slammed into the ground seconds later and rolled several times before grinding to a halt, somehow ending up on its wheels.

"Are you injured?" Hain questioned from atop the chancellor. The car's armor and inertial damping technology had protected the passengers, but the older man's worn-down condition necessitated greater scrutiny.

"I'm fine," Macey gasped.

"Stay here," Hain ordered. He then crawled to the door where he pulled the emergency release which fired the explosive bolts and threw the door away from the vehicle.

After climbing out, the agent turned towards the city and froze in place. Curious as to what could cause a trained agent to freeze up like that, Macey ignored the danger and made his way to the door and followed the agent's gaze, then felt his own jaw drop in shock at the sight.

Not even the empire would do such a thing.

Yet it had.

Blue Fire Fortress
10:23 A.M.

"No!" Colonel Leon Tyquese cried out. A fiery mushroom cloud filled the screen in front of him, taking the place of the capital city. There were millions of people in that city, including his own parents.

Instinct burned within him to run down to the garage, grab a vehicle, and drive to the city as fast as possible to do something — anything — but he remained in place. He was obligated to do his duty, and there wasn't anything he could do out there anyway. His parents were nothing but vapor now.

His outcry caused General Reno to look up at the screen and curse the empire upon seeing the blossoming mushroom cloud.

"Blue Fire, this is Panther detail! Convoy hit by shockwave and disabled! Request immediate assistance!"

"Hold on, Panther. Help is on the way," Tyquese responded, using training and experience to push aside his feelings and do his job.

"Send Team One with Alpha Wing," Reno ordered, and the colonel immediately complied. Both groups were fast response units, with Team One being infantry and Alpha Wing as flyers. The infantry would evac the convoy personnel while the flyers watched their backs.

"We've got incoming!"

"They're going straight for the convoy!"

"Roger command. We're on afterburners," Alpha Leader responded.

"Under heavy attack! Where's that support!?" Panther called in.

"ETA, forty seconds," Tyquese responded.

Unintelligible shouting filled the line, then there was only silence.

"Panther, report!" Reno demanded.

Silence.

"No way they got in and out that fast!"

"Convoy is in sight. Several Ordonian small craft fleeing the scene. In pursuit."

"Engage at your discretion, Alpha," Reno ordered.

"Roger, Command."

"Captain Jens, Team One, on scene. Panther detail is dead, and Chancellor Macey is missing."

The command center fell silent as they watched the tactical screen where Alpha Wing was closing in on the enemy craft, but they could see they didn't have enough time.

"Targets are nearly within weapons range of their fleet ships. We are unable to intercept them before that happens. Please advise, Command."

"Return to base," Reno sighed, his voice heavy with fatigue.

"What are we going to do now?"

Upon not hearing a response, Tyquese looked at the general to see him staring at the image of the mushroom cloud in silence, so he decided to say something himself.

"We fight, and keep fighting, until we can fight no more."

Chapter One
The Beginning of The End

Vehla
Blue Fire Fortress
Wednesday, December 11th, 2707
6:03 A.M.

The colonel stood at the hangar's main door and watched the white plasma orbs raining down in the distance.

One year ago, the Ordeon Empire secured orbital control of the planet and swore it would never stop its bombardment until the people surrendered. Even after all this time, they still didn't understand the power of freedom and the determination of the Vehlan Union to secure and defend that right for all people.

His gaze shifted toward the ground to a blur of light marking the location of the Ordonian siege base erected in the ruins of the union capital. The nuclear weapon which had destroyed the city left behind little radiation, leaving it wide open for them to move in and build atop the ashes of Vehlan citizens, including his own parents. He'd kept his promise to keep fighting, but the fortress in which he now stood was all that remained of a great nation.

The two nations had been sworn enemies for all of recorded history, and no one alive today knew how it had all started. One-hundred years ago, the hatred erupted into war once again, but this time both sides vowed they would not stop until the other was destroyed. So the fighting continued, year after year, decade after decade, with neither side gaining a clear advantage over the other.

That changed three years ago when the current emperor ascended the Ordonian throne. He quickly introduced radical new tactics which caught the Vehlans off-guard and left them guessing as to his next move.

When he attacked Vehla, the union pulled in as many ships as it could in the attempt to free its home world, but the emperor was ready for them and defeated them every time. With the defenses in the other union systems now weakened, the Imps moved in and captured them one by one.

Every morning, he stood here and asked himself why he kept fighting, why he continued to lead others in a hopeless struggle. Some days it took longer than others, but he always came around to the conclusion that tyranny cannot be allowed to thrive and someone had to stand against it, no matter what.

His resolve renewed once more, the colonel turned his back on the sights of war and walked back through the hangar, his footsteps echoing in the emptiness. The few remaining fighter craft, damaged beyond their ability to repair them, were not enough to silence the reminder of all they had lost.

When he stepped out and into the corridor, he encountered a pair of armored soldiers on the way to their duty station. They looked at him long enough to raise their right hand to helmet rim in salute, an action he reciprocated with hand to forehead while wishing he could say or do something to lift their spirits, but there wasn't anything. He was the adjutant to the union's top general, but he felt just as powerless as the enlisted man serving on the front lines.

The open faces of their helmets revealed one of them to have a light complexion, marking him as a non-native of Vehla, yet here he was fighting alongside the dark-skinned natives such as Leon to save their civilization. A perfect example of the union's diverse unity in action.

He continued on his way to the command center, and upon entering found General Reno standing with his hands behind his back, staring at a tactical screen.

"The Ordonians are normally preparing to attack by now, but this morning they are quiet," the general observed.

"One of our snipers reported a hit on their commander yesterday. He's either dead or critically injured, and they won't attack without him," Colonel Tyquese responded.

"I don't think that's the reason. Our observers just reported several enemy troop ships landing at their base in United. They've been using these constant attacks the last two weeks to probe our defenses and learn exactly what they need to breach them. Now they are preparing for a final strike."

"What's your plan?"

"We're going to move as many personnel as possible to the wall, leaving minimum numbers at the other positions," Reno dictated, pointing at the relevant positions on the map as he spoke without relaxing his stiff posture.

The colonel paused to consider the plan, studying the map and visualizing the proposed movements as he thought.

Blue Fire Fortress was conceived as a bunker to house and protect government officials in the event of a planetary siege, and the dormant supervolcano several miles to the east of the capital seemed an ideal location.

The main bunker was built into a mountain on the east end of the caldera, the result of a more recent, smaller eruption. Lava flows combined with seismic activity had created a ring of sheer cliffs, extending from the mountain and bordering the north and south sides of the caldera. There were few routes an army could take through the cliffs, and the Vehlans had a defense station on the caldera side of each one.

Only the western edge was open, but a fortified wall was built to seal it off. There was nothing in the caldera itself, but it was often used as a training or assembly area. Underground tunnels allowed for the safe movement of personnel and equipment, but the whole facility was also protected by magnetic deflection shields and interceptor weaponry.

"What makes you so sure they'll be attacking the wall?" Tyquese asked. He trusted his superior's considerable experience and expertise, but it was his job to gauge each situation for himself and draw his own conclusions.

"That is where they have attacked every day for the past two weeks, each time with greater strength. We must conclude that they were probing it to learn how much they needed to breach it. Now that their reinforcements have arrived, they are ready to move, and we must be prepared to repel them," the general explained matter-of-factly.

"We can't be certain of that. I recommend we keep the garrisons as they are. The wall can hold with its current numbers, and there's always the chance they will attack from multiple directions. We can always reinforce the wall later if necessary," Tyquese respectfully disagreed.

"Ordonians always prefer brute force over clever tactics. They will attack the wall with everything they have, and there may not be enough time to transfer units after combat begins. We need to move them now so we can repel the attack when it comes, and then we can move them back afterwards."

"They caught us unprepared with a change in tactics before, sir. We must be wary of them doing so again if we are to have any hope of enduring."

For the first time since the colonel had entered, Reno turned away from the tactical screen to look him in the eyes.

"I have been fighting the empire for a long time, *Colonel*. I know them better than anyone, and I know what they are going to do next. Now follow my orders and redeploy those troops," he demanded.

It was clear he wasn't going to change his mind, but Leon knew this was a mistake. The amount of troops they had seen the enemy bringing in were enough to breach the wall in a frontal assault, but they were also enough to launch powerful attacks from multiple directions. It was also possible the Ordonians were landing troops and equipment where they couldn't see, then bringing them in over land.

He had to follow the general's orders, but he also had a responsibility to defend this base and somehow find a way to turn the tide of the war. There was only one option that would allow him to do both in this situation.

"Request temporary transfer to Outpost Three, sir."

"Request denied. Your place is here."

"My place is with my troops, fighting the enemy. It's time I took it."

The general studied him for a moment, in a way that seemed as though he were trying to remember a feeling he'd known once, but had forgotten under the burdens of command.

He finally approved the request, and Leon raised his right hand to forehead in salute before turning and leaving the room.

Victory Siege Base
7:00 A.M.

The transport ramp finished lowering and Legion Commander Max Canza placed himself at the top, his breath turning to fog in the cold as he resisted the urge to rub his eyes where the recently inserted contact lenses could still be felt. They were necessary for him to see clearly in the dim light of the Vehlan sun, which never lit the planet any brighter than a clear night on his own world of Ordeos. It could explain why the Vehlans were such depressing people.

A burning sensation on his face prompted him to raise a gloved hand to shield the exposed skin from the sunlight. It may appear dark to him, but this belied the fact it was a high-energy star which quickly burned his tan but light skin relative to the planet's natives.

The sound of perfectly-timed marching filled the air, and the commander scanned the landing area as thousands of Ordonian troops in dark red armor debarked their landing craft, the flags held by the front lines flapping in the breeze generated by their determined pace and casting shadowy reflections across their mirrored faceshields.

Thousands of troops had landed here, and thousands more were landing at other locations further away, far from the prying eyes of the Vehlan sentries at their stronghold. The time to end this seemingly endless war had arrived at last, and it was his honor to lead his people to victory. A victory which would finally allow them to raise up all humans from chaos into the paradise envisioned by the empire.

As the soldiers assembled in the gathering area to await bunk assignments, the commander chose to savor the moment by taking a look at his surroundings. The siege base sat in the middle of what used to be the Vehlan capital, built where the nuclear device had vaporized everything. There was no lingering danger from the detonation as engineers had long ago found a way to construct such weapons that didn't emit harmful radiation.

Many buildings on the edges of the city had survived the detonation, but were still heavily damaged by the shockwave and fires. What had once stood as a symbol of the union's diversity and unity was now nothing but rubble and dust. It was fitting that the last vestiges of the troublesome nation would be destroyed by an army marching from these ruins.

Satisfied that all was going according to plan, Canza finally made his way down the ramp to find a lieutenant waiting for him at the bottom.

When he drew near, the man snapped to attention and saluted by placing his right fist over his heart.

"Where is Farra?" Canza snapped, returning the salute and walking past without missing a step. The lieutenant fell into step beside him before answering.

"Legion Captain Farra is in the infirmary, sir. He chose to lead yesterday's attack from the front line and was injured by an enemy sniper. The doctor reports that his injuries are not severe, but the captain has decided not to return to duty and remain in the infirmary."

"Understood. See to the needs of the new arrivals. Dismissed," Canza responded.

He made his way to the prefabricated base hospital which was one of the first buildings assembled after their arrival on the planet. The armored guards offered no reaction as he passed, and soon he was standing just past the door to the main ward watching the nurses tend the patients in beds with scanner panels on either side while the doctors monitored them from a row of computers to the left of the entrance.

The chief medical officer noticed him almost immediately and approached him with a salute and report.

"Sir, Legion Captain Farra's physical condition is stable. I fear for his emotional stability; however, as he has refused to leave his bed and is hardly eating or drinking."

"Where is he?"

"I put him in a private room. This way."

The doctor led him to the far end of the beds, then turned left and went through a door. Upon entering the room, Canza spotted his second-in-command lying on a bed in the center with a nurse attending him.

"Leave us," he commanded, and the doctor and nurse immediately vacated the room, closing the door behind them.

"I failed you, Legion Commander," Farra spoke first while avoiding the gaze of his superior.

“Look at me.”

“That would be inappropriate, sir. My failure makes me unworthy.”

“I gave you an order. I expect you to obey.”

Farra hesitated a moment, then turned to face the commander, but kept his brown eyes directed towards the floor.

“Explain to me how you failed.”

“My mission was to breach the enemy defenses, and I did not do so. All I managed to do was to get hundreds of our people killed.”

“I never ordered you to breach their defenses,” Canza declared, causing his subordinate to finally look at him with surprise.

“I don't understand. Why else would you order me to continuously attack during your absence?”

“The daily reports indicate you attacked the wall at least once a day, in different sections and with varying degrees of power. This doubtless led them to believe we were testing the quality of their defenses in preparation for a major strike, a belief no doubt solidified by my arriving today with considerable reinforcements.”

“You are preparing a trap for them?”

“Precisely.”

“I didn't know that, sir. I apologize if it appeared I was doubting you.”

“Your own ambition clouded your senses and prevented you from determining the larger strategy. As my permanent executive officer, you will be required to mend this flaw,” Canza responded, eliciting another shocked expression.

“Your permanent...?”

“Yes. I need someone in whose loyalty I can have absolute faith, and your actions have proven you are that person. The future holds many more campaigns for me, and I want you to be at my side for them,” Canza explained.

The legion captain vaulted out of the bed and snapped off a salute, his injured pride forgotten and wounded body ignored.

“You honor me, sir, and I promise to never fail you.”

Canza returned the salute, then called for the doctor.

"I want this man discharged immediately. He has much work to do in preparation for tomorrow's attack."

Chapter Two
A Planet Falls

Outpost Three
Thursday, December 12th, 2707
6:42 A.M.

Alarms sounded, blasting through the weary silence of the mostly empty cafeteria. Utensils and plates clattered as the breakfasting soldiers bolted from their seats and hustled to their battle stations.

Colonel Tyquese rushed into the outpost's command station and quickly checked that all positions were manned and ready. When he was sure that all was well at this outpost, he turned his attention to the tactical screen for the whole fortress and saw a large enemy army marching on the wall.

The assault force comprised several thousand foot-soldiers with the empire's heavy, dual cannon Atlas Tanks in front and on both sides. These behemoths sat atop a pair of treads capable of crushing most barriers and had a crew of five.

Overhead circled Carnage class ground support gunships bristling with weapons on the fuselage and wings while a small escort of dagger shaped light fighters flew around their perimeter, just in case the Vehlan defenders still had fighter craft in reserve, which they didn't.

Two-thousand Vehlan soldiers were in place to defend the wall, while another thousand garrisoned the various outposts around the caldera's edge. They were greatly outnumbered, but the gun emplacements and barricades protecting them were enough to even the odds.

The power arrayed against them was impressive, but so far it was only directed against the wall, which should hold given the reinforcements General Reno had moved there the day before. However, Leon still wasn't convinced this was all there was to the enemy plan.

For now, all he could do was watch and wait.

And hope.

Ordonian Attack Formation
6:56 A.M.

From his position near the front of the infantry formation, Private James Menza watched as the enemy fortress came into view. A feeling of minor disappointment spread through him when he realized there was nothing but a simple wall between them and victory.

Is this how the Nihls have thwarted our attacks for nearly a year? he wondered as they drew closer, referencing his enemy by their slang name which was short for Nihilists. The Vehlans were anarchists who were nothing compared to the Ordonians, making it a fitting term.

This may only be his first battle, but as he drew closer even he could tell that this so-called fortress was nothing compared to the might of the imperial army.

Whatever the reason was, he was glad for the opportunity to play a part in the final defeat of his people's most hated enemy.

The tanks and soldiers halted their march while the gunships ceased their circling and came together in attack formation, then raced towards the wall, filling the air with the roar of their engines.

At the same time, the Atlas tanks opened fire with their plasma cannons and rocket launchers, shaking the ground with each shot.

The burning white plasma lit up the stony field as the soldiers broke out cheering.

Blue Fire Defensive Wall
7:03 A.M.

Several dozen hostile gunships sped towards them, but Private Eric Olian held his ground. No matter how bad things became, he was a Union soldier, and he would not run.

The first volley from the Imp tanks reached them before the gunships did, but the plasma shots were dispersed by the magnetic shield while the rockets were easily destroyed by the interceptors.

The gunships entered weapons range and unleashed a volley of rockets while the base's anti-air weaponry also opened fire.

This time there were too many rockets for the interceptors to stop them all, and one managed to strike the wall below Olian, nearly knocking him off his feet with the resulting explosion, but he was unharmed.

Two more rockets flew over the wall nearby and impacted the ground on the other side, but didn't cause any damage.

Meanwhile, the Vehlan weapons scored several direct hits on the planes, downing a few and damaging others enough to force them to turn back. But now the rest were close enough to use all their weapons, and they began firing with their rapid-fire plasma guns in addition to the rockets, the magnetic shield doing no good at this range. These weapons were almost useless against the entrenched guns, but the soldiers atop the wall were another matter.

The gunships strafed the wall while the soldiers scrambled out of the way. Some returned fire, but most resisted in the interest of conserving ammo with the knowledge there was little chance of causing any damage.

Screams filled the air along with the smell of burnt flesh, but training and experience kept Olian from succumbing to fear as he sought to help the wounded and stay alive.

Outpost Three
7:09 A.M.

Casualty numbers automatically estimated by the tactical computer appeared on the screen as Colonel Tyquese watched. Loss of life was never a good thing, but so far things were going better than he had expected.

Movement elsewhere on the screen caught his attention, and he looked back at the Ordonian ground formation to see it had resumed its advance. This should have been cause for alarm, but the defenders were ready for them.

New symbols appeared on the screen as dozens of Vehlan Missile Tanks emerged from the tunnels in the caldera. Several of the attacking gunships turned away from the wall to deal with this new threat, but all were targeted and shot down before they could do anything.

Then the enemy formation came within range, and General Reno's voice came over the comms to seal their fate.

"Missile tanks open fire."

Ordonian Attack Formation
7:24 A.M.

Now that the gunships had softened up the Vehlan defenses, the order was given to resume marching.

The sound of weapons fire grew louder as they approached, but the shouts and screams of the defenders also became audible. For the first time, Menza felt a flicker of fear and hesitation enter his heart. He was ready to do his duty for the empire and put an end to their enemy, but he wasn't ready to die. What if the Vehlans were stronger than they appeared and he was killed before having the chance to accomplish anything?

His heart skipped a beat when he saw a wing of five gunships break off their attack and head back towards them at full-speed as if something had frightened them.

The fortress focused its anti-air batteries on them, shooting down three of them before they could get out of range. Somehow the fleeing gunships were more of a threat to the Vehlans than those attacking, and Menza felt his mouth go dry as the realization he could be marching to his death finally sunk in.

Then the panicked voice of one of the fleeing pilots came through on all frequencies, and his training was all that kept the private moving forward.

"Do not advance! Union Missile Tanks behind wall! Large formation! Our signal is being jammed! Please signal upon receipt of message!"

The warning came too late.

Dozens of missiles powerful enough to be used in space combat arced up and away from the fortress, then swooped down towards the front line of tanks.

There was no cover and no chance of getting out of the way, so the formation halted and opened fire on the incoming missiles, hoping to destroy them in the air. They stopped many of them, but would never get them all, and another volley was already in the air.

The first volley struck, destroying several tanks in terrible explosions and sending soldiers flying in every direction like leaves in the wind.

Menza took aim at a missile coming his general direction, but it was too fast for him and it struck its target.

The tank a couple dozen feet in front of him exploded, and the resulting shockwave sent him flying.

He spun in the air, and as he saw the ground rapidly approaching, he couldn't help but wonder if his first battle had also become his last.

Victory Siege Base
7:43 A.M.

Legion Commander Canza smiled inwardly when he saw the enemy missiles, but was careful to maintain his emotionless facial expression. The enemy thought this would be their salvation, but it was only the final step in their slow march to oblivion.

"Send in the second wave. Remaining assault forces move into attack position," he ordered.

A squadron of fifty flying-wing bombers roared by overhead, followed closely by a hundred more gunships. They would take care of those Vehlan Missile Tanks while transports carrying enough Ordonian Atlas Tanks and soldiers to replace all those lost came in behind them.

Blue Fire Defensive Wall
7:51 A.M.

The attack waned, and Eric Olian dared to expose himself long enough to take a look at the enemy ground formation, and felt his heart skip a beat when he saw the destruction wrought by the missile tanks. The battle would be over soon. They had managed to endure another day.

His limbs suddenly felt heavy, so he leaned back against the barrier and closed his eyes.

Cheers from the remaining Ordonian soldiers cut short his repose, and he gripped his rifle tight as fresh adrenaline flooded his system. He leaned to his right to see around the barricade, then froze solid when he saw what had evoked the cheers.

Hundreds of bombers were descending through the sparse clouds, and just as many gunships were heading towards them from the direction of the capital. The base's anti-air weapons shifted their focus from the first wave of gunships to the incoming bombers, but it was too little, too late.

A few of the bombers were shot down, but the rest made it through the barrage and opened fire with their missiles, quickly destroying the fortified weapons.

Many of them then began targeting the emitters for the deflection shield while the rest went straight for the Missile Tanks. Eric didn't see what happened next as he was more concerned with the gunships headed for the wall.

Not caring how little his chances were of causing damage, he climbed to his feet and opened fire on those planes while screaming at the top of his lungs.

Then he saw one headed straight for him, its rotary cannon already spewing plasma fire. There wasn't enough time to dodge to either side, nor was there any viable cover, so he dropped his rifle then turned and ran off the wall into empty air.

The gunship passed by, barely missing him, but there was still the ground for him to deal with.

He'd had the foresight to jump sideways, allowing him to land on his side and go into a roll to reduce injury, but he was still rolling when his world went dark.

Outpost Three
8:13 A.M.

"The deflection shield and anti-air defenses at the wall are gone. Recommend we pull back and ambush them when they enter the caldera," Colonel Tyquese advised the general via comlink. These developments were not unexpected, a fact which helped him to remain calm.

"Negative. Reinforce the wall using personnel from the outposts. We have to stop them there," Reno responded.

"That would leave our flanks virtually undefended, sir!"

"Protecting our flanks won't do us any good if we lose the wall! Move those troops!"

He still didn't like it, but Leon obeyed his C.O. and arranged for as many soldiers as possible to relocate to the wall.

As he watched the relevant symbols on the tactical screen move into the tunnels, he couldn't help but wonder if there was really any point. Even if they managed to turn back this attack, they were still surrounded and alone. Why keep fighting at all?

Then he recalled the sight of a mushroom cloud expanding above United, and he grit his teeth as he looked at the screen with renewed determination.

They fought because they must, and he would find a way to turn it all around.

For them.

All of them.

Victory Siege Base
8:22 A.M.

The scouts Canza had assigned to watch the enemy flanks reported many of the Vehlan defenders vacating their posts, presumably leaving to go reinforce the main wall. The sensors on his ships in orbit should have been able to give him more details, but the Vehlans were using jamming technology they had thus far been unable to find a way to circumvent.

"Sir, with the battle going so well, I have a question I would like to ask," Legion Captain Farra spoke up.

"Go ahead."

"This large-scale attack is working perfectly, so why have you only used small attacks before now?"

"One cannot take a fortress like this without an intimate understanding of its defenses, and the minds of those defending it. The first assault was much like this one, and thousands of our people were killed in the attempt. That's when command of the siege was transferred to me, and I don't make those kinds of mistakes," Canza explained.

"So you never expected those other attacks to succeed?"

The legion commander's only response was a short nod.

"What about all those who died?"

"There were less casualties in all those attacks combined than there were in that first one alone, and there will be less now because I know exactly what needs to be done. Victory is finally within our grasp, and we owe it all to their sacrifice."

Outpost Three
8:49 A.M.

"Stay alert!" Tyquese shouted, and the corporal staring towards the wall jerked his attention back to the gulley leading through the cliffs.

Fearing an attack was imminent, the colonel had abandoned the tactical screen and taken position on the perimeter with the command center directly behind him. He was maintaining an aura of alert calm for his soldiers, but he was feeling the same worry as the man at whom he'd just shouted. The sounds of battle coming from the wall continued to grow in intensity, eating away at his resolve and sense of duty.

"Enemy sighted!" someone shouted just before a volley of white plasma bolts erupted from the gulley.

"Return fire! Keep them pinned down!" Tyquese shouted before opening fire himself.

They filled the gulley with red lasers, forcing the Ordonians to stay in cover with few openings to shoot back. The defenders were able to keep this up for several minutes, but then an attacker managed to fire a rocket which struck the main fortification which sent debris and people flying.

Attacking soldiers rushed into the resulting gap in cover fire, firing as they came. Several were struck down, but the rest continued to gain ground.

Tyquese ducked behind a barricade, pulled out a detonator, and pressed the small screen on the side. The device instantly synced with his armor's onboard computer to verify his identity, then set off the explosives on either side of the gulley.

He watched the reflection in the metal surface before him as rocks and boulders rained down on the imps, killing many of them and blocking the way for the rest.

Or at least that was the plan.

The colonel raised himself up just enough to see over the top of the barricade, and felt his strength evaporate with the last of his hope at what he saw.

Dozens of enemy soldiers were clambering over the rubble, ignoring their dead and wounded and stubbornly rushing into the faltering defense.

"Fall back! To the tunnel!" he ordered, then laid down cover fire so those at the front could get away.

A rocket flew past him and struck the command center wall, the resulting explosion shoving him flat to the ground.

His eyesight became hazy as the world swirled around him, but a fellow soldier pulled him up before he lost consciousness and half-dragged him down the back stairs.

His vision cleared as they were entering the tunnel at the center of the base, and he pulled away from the soldier to turn and see if anyone else was coming. He saw no one, but heard dozens of booted feet running towards him and voices speaking in Ordonian, so he pressed his hand against a pad on the wall, triggering the explosives at the entrance and sealing it off.

Blue Fire Defensive Wall
9:04 A.M.

"Eric!"

The voice came from far away, as if from a dream. It sounded familiar, but he couldn't quite put a name to it. Why would someone be yelling at him, what was he doing here, and what was the deal with all that noise?

Then a dull ache in his entire body and a sharp pain on his forehead brought it all rushing back, and he opened his eyes to discover he was lying face down in the dirt. Groaning, he slowly pushed himself up with one arm, but was about to fall down again when someone grabbed him and pulled him up.

"There you are! We have to get out of here!"

"What happened?" Eric asked as the owner of the familiar voice supported his weight and began walking the two of them away from the wall as fast as he could.

He managed to lift his head long enough to look around, and saw everyone running away. Some were heading for the tunnels, while others elected to run into the open caldera past the burning wrecks of the missile tanks.

"Looks like you hit your head on a rock. Why you would do something like that is beyond me."

"Why don't they put face protection on these helmets again?"

"Something about how they restrict peripheral vision," his friend, who he now recognized as Private Jeremy Fields, responded.

"Makes sense," he grumbled as Jeremy led him into a tunnel.

Ordonian Attack Formation
9:12 A.M.

Private Menza opened his eyes to see a medic leaning over him and pocketing a used injector.

"You were rendered unconscious by a nearby explosion but are uninjured. The stimulant I just gave you is all you need to get back in the fight," the medic hurriedly explained, then rushed away to his next patient.

The private rolled onto his side, then pushed himself to his feet. As he did, he noticed dozens of his fellow soldiers running towards the enemy base, cheering as they went.

He looked where they were headed, and any residual feeling of sluggishness evaporated instantly upon the sight of several gaps in the main wall and the remaining nihls either fleeing or surrendering.

A triumphant cheer burst forth from his lungs, and he charged forward with all the speed he could muster.

In his haste to rejoin the battle, and thus partake in the imminent victory, he neglected to recover his rifle. When he noticed his oversight, he slid to a stop and frantically looked around for it. There was no telling where it had ended up, but he spotted another one nearby, so he scooped it up and resumed his charge.

Blue Fire Command Center
9:19 A.M.

The first thing Colonel Tyquese noticed upon rushing into the command center was the flurry of activity as section commanders struggled to find some way to stop the enemy advance. One look at the screens dashed any hopes for success as the red enemy icons were flooding through every possible opening while the blue icons of their own forces were fleeing before them.

Next, he noticed the general seated in the center of the room leaning forward with his face buried in both hands. Defeat was written all over him, but Leon marched up to him and saluted regardless.

"Orders, sir?"

There was no response at first, but then Reno finally lifted his head, then stood to look the colonel in the eyes as he straightened his uniform.

"Execute emergency evacuation. Lead whoever is left to safety wherever you can find it. This planet, and our nation, may fall to the enemy, but the fight for freedom must never end."

"Emergency evacuation! All personnel to the transports!" Tyquese shouted.

Alarms sounded, a pre-recorded voice came over the intercoms telling people to abandon the base, and those in the command center scrambled to destroy sensitive material.

"Are you not coming with us, sir?" Leon questioned.

"No. I have fought this war for too long, and have become blind to what needs to be done. I see now that you are better equipped to lead this fight, but there is one more thing you need to know," Reno responded as he pulled a notebook from his pocket.

"My predecessor gave me a book my first day on the job, but it was destroyed in the empire's attack on the capital. I have written down all I could remember, and now I pass that information on to you," he explained as he handed over the notebook.

The colonel accepted it, but then stared at it as if unsure what to do with it.

"Yes, it is paper. Once you read it, you will understand that such things should not be stored electronically where they are easily copied and stolen. Now leave."

Leon finally tucked the small pad into a zippered pocket on the front of his armor, then snapped off a final salute and exited the command center behind the last operator.

Underground Tunnel
9:22 A.M.

"Abandon base! Repeat, abandon base! This is not a drill! All units to escape transports immediately! Abandon base!"

"What's the point? Where are we going to go?" Private Eric Olian despaired as he limped beside his friend.

"We will go where we can fight to free our people. Now hurry up, will ya? I'm not about to eat Imp plasma just because you found out you can't fly!"

A sarcastic response came to Eric's mind, but he chose to ignore it and instead focused on moving as fast as possible.

They finally made it to the hangar and boarded a transport, and were just settling into their seats when Colonel Tyquese himself ran up the ramp and straight to the cockpit. They exchanged surprised glances at his bloody and dusty form, but kept any remarks to themselves.

Vehlan Escape Ship
9:41 A.M.

"Take off now," Leon ordered as he sat in the co-pilot's seat.

"There are still people coming," the pilot protested.

"No, there isn't. Those who are left are surrounded and soon it will be Ordonians flooding into this hangar rather than our own people. We have to launch now."

The pilot hesitated, but then he relayed the launch order to the other ships, closed the doors to his craft, and opened the main hangar doors.

A loud hum filled the cabin as the transport powered its engines, and it grew in volume as the levels neared full.

The pilot finally activated the engines, and the passengers were pressed into their seats as the craft shot out of the hangar at high speed. Dampers protected them from the worst of the g-forces, but nothing could fully prevent their effects at this rate of acceleration.

They moved beyond the range of any planetary resistance well before the Ordonians could react, but that still left the orbital blockade for them to get past. Normally a planet was too large to effectively blockade, but since the Vehlans only controlled one site from which to launch any ships, this section of space was locked down tight.

The transports broke out of the atmosphere a few minutes later, and Leon soon saw on the screen the enemy ships closing in on them. A safe jump into hyperspace required a certain distance from a planetary body and other ships, and the Ordonians were determined to ensure they never achieved that distance.

Volleys of plasma fire shot towards them, but the pilot hit the boosters and deftly maneuvered his way through the projectiles and then past the ships firing them.

Safely in open space, he powered the hyperdrive and took them into hyperspace.

"How many made it?" Leon asked.

The pilot checked in with the rest of the convoy, then replied that all the transports had made it through with only minor damage.

"At least that much went right for us," he commented, then ordered the convoy to drop out of hyperspace around the last planet in the system, an uninhabited world of no concern to the empire.

Their home was now fully under imperial control. All they could do now was wait and see what happened next.

Imperial Dreadnaught
OES Thunderstrike
9:59 A.M.

"Follow them into hyperspace, sir?" Helm questioned.

"Negative. They aren't important. Resume blockade pattern," Captain Alvise Zenzal ordered.

Chasing and/or fighting someone in hyperspace was a difficult proposition, an effort wasted on hunting down a few transports full of refugees.

As the ship settled back into parking orbit, the captain stared at the planet on the main screen. It seemed hardly worth all the effort to capture it, but at least it was all over now.

Not just one battle, but the whole war.

All of it.

Chapter Three
A New Regime

United
Thursday, December 12th, 2707
4:59 P.M.

The bars slid into the wall on the right with a soft hiss, and both guards violently shoved General Reno into the cell. He barely had enough time to put out his arms to prevent himself from faceplanting the opposite wall, then he quickly spun around intending to let loose at the Ordonians with profanities if nothing else, but they grabbed him again before he could do anything.

He was forced into a sitting position, then chained to the wall. When they were satisfied he wasn't going anywhere, the fully-armored soldiers took up positions on either side of the door, facing him with rifles held across their chests.

While he waited for whatever happened next, the general chose to survey his surroundings. He was in an underground cell with small windows near the ceiling, through which the setting sun provided the only light. It was about three by four meters and covered in filth stinking of acrid water, a dungeon befitting the Imp penchant for overdone theatrics.

He normally avoided even thinking the slang term used by the common soldier for their enemy, a shortening of imperial which denoted their nefarious nature, but maintaining appearances hardly seemed worthwhile given his current circumstances.

As his eyes adjusted to the gloom, he realized he wasn't the only prisoner when he spotted a battered form sitting in the corner to his right. He squinted at the gaunt, balding man staring at his hands in his lap, and finally recognized him as Chancellor Landon Macey, the rightfully elected leader of the Vehlan Union.

"The two of you are all that remains of the Vehlan Union. You failed to save your nation, and the Ordeon Empire reigns victorious. There is no more reason to fight," a voice stated from the doorway, and Reno turned to see an imperial Legion Commander with the name Canza pinned on his immaculate uniform of faded red khaki pants and jacket with black shirt and boots.

"Freedom for all people, and bringing tyrants to justice are reason enough to fight, but you wouldn't understand that," Reno countered.

"How are your people served by continuing to fight for failed ideologies?"

"Why does it matter? We have nothing left to fight you with even if we wanted, as you have already seen fit to point out."

"There are always those who will continue to resist as long as they believe there is still something to salvage. Issue the surrender order, disband what remains of your military, and submit to Ordonian rule. This will show your people that the war is truly over so we can begin to rebuild in peace, and ensure a safe future for everyone," the commander proposed, causing Reno to snort derisive laughter.

"Your idea of rebuilding is to make us into slaves, and no one is safe so long as the Ordeon Empire exists," he retorted.

The commander stared at him dispassionately, then glanced at the chancellor before stating they had an hour to decide, after which he left the room with the guards right behind him.

"Is it true there is nothing left?" Macey asked without looking up.

"No, it isn't. A few thousand of our soldiers escaped the planet before the Ordonians could secure the fortress."

"What good are a few thousand against the hundreds of millions in the Ordonian military?"

"I trust their commander and believe if anyone can find a way to turn this around, it is him," Reno insisted. He was careful not to reveal Leon's name in the event their captors were listening, but was confident the rest of what he was saying wouldn't do them any good.

The chancellor didn't respond and still hadn't even looked at him, so he just leaned against the wall and hoped the leader of free people still had the willpower to resist dictators.

Jail Cell
6:05 P.M.

The cell door slid open, and Canza stepped inside to find his prisoners the same as when he left. Reno glared at him while Macey sat slumped in his corner, staring at the floor.

"It is time to decide. Will you do what is best for your people, or will you choose to prolong their suffering?"

"What is best for *your* people you mean," Reno jabbed.

"Unending conflict destroys everyone's lives, but cooperation allows us to grow to ever greater heights. All those living in the former union territories will become citizens of the empire, and your public submission will make for a smooth and speedy transition."

"Is that supposed to be a good thing?"

An exasperated sigh rose within Canza, but he suppressed it before even a hint of it could reveal itself to the others in the room.

"I will not continue to banter with you, Reno. You are defeated. Accept that and allow both our people to move on, or continue in your denial and risk dragging this out for another hundred years."

"Go jump out an airlock."

"Are those your feelings as well, Chancellor?"

Macey let out a long, low sigh, then slowly rose to his feet and looked into the commander's eyes.

"All wars end eventually. This one has lasted so long that war is all we have ever known. The final outcome is not what I desired, but it is what has transpired, and it is time for us to know peace.

"I will do as you ask," he stated.

"You can't do that! We can't give in to these tyrants!" Reno shouted.

"Quiet! You had your say and your chance," Canza rebuked, then ordered the guards to release Macey's chains and bring him with them.

They did as they were told, leaving the general shouting after them with pleas to the chancellor to not give up, which soon gave way to insults directed towards the Ordonians.

He wouldn't be an issue for much longer.

Jail Cell
Friday, December 13th, 2707
6:53 A.M.

The dawn crept into the underground cell to show the general leaning against the wall, his chin on his chest and hands on the floor. Exhaustion had forced him to cease shouting sometime during the night, but sleep had never come.

All his life he had fought to uphold and advance the ideals of the Vehlan Union. He had sent millions of soldiers to their deaths in the defense of individual freedom and self-determination, and they went because they trusted him to protect their nation and their loved ones. They trusted him to ensure their sacrifice was not without meaning.

He had failed.

His only consolation was that he could face whatever came next with the knowledge he had stood with his people and their ideals until the very end. If only the chancellor were doing the same, instead of betraying them and handing them over to the enemy.

The door opened, and he looked up to see four Star Knights charging into the cell. Two of them released his chains, then the other two hauled him to his feet. One of the first two took up position in front of him while the other brought up the rear, then they dragged him out of the cell.

He briefly considered fighting back if for no other reason than to be a nuisance, but he realized there was nothing he could do against a knight and chose to cooperate.

They stopped at the entrance to the cell block long enough for the knights to sign out their prisoner. Then, they led him into the lobby through which a dozen soldiers had formed a path by standing at attention down the center. Upon finally exiting the building, he was led up some steps to stand at the back of a prefabricated stage, the knights taking up position around him.

On the stage with him was Legion Commander Canza in a black suit with red stripes running down the length of the arms and legs and a mahogany shirt with black tie which served as the dress uniform for the top tier officers of the Ordonian military. Next to him was Chancellor Macey, recently bathed and dressed in a fresh dark blue suit.

What used to be a plaza, probably for a hotel, stretched out in front of them and it was currently filled with union citizens. He could see four Urban Suppression Mechs standing guard on the crowd's perimeter, four and a half meter tall human shaped vehicles minus a head designed specifically for crowd control. Escorts of five armored soldiers each stood around them, their armor a faded red color due to the adaptive camouflage being turned off, while behind them were piles of rubble, all that remained of the once beautiful Vehlan capital.

With the blue Vehlan sun rising before him, Macey stepped up to the podium at the front of the stage. He glanced at the screen in the center, most likely reviewing a prepared speech, and Reno stepped forward to stop him, but he was prevented from taking any action when the knight on his left grabbed his arm and leaned in to whisper in his ear.

"If you cause a disturbance, our soldiers will kill every last person in that plaza. You will watch, and then you will die."

What the chancellor was about to do was wrong, but he couldn't allow all those people to be slaughtered, so he remained silent and awaited the inevitable.

"One hundred years of war came to an end yesterday when the last military stronghold of the Vehlan Union was seized by Ordonian forces. Our military is destroyed, our world lies in ruins, and the empire is victorious.

"I know many of you believe that we can still fight, and that we should. You believe that if we never give up, we will one day find a way to defeat our enemy and restore our nation. These were my thoughts as well, but I was encouraged to consider what is best for my people, for you, and I have come to the belief it is time for the fighting to end. We have lost much, including the ability to build a future for ourselves, and continued conflict will only make things worse.

"So, in the interest of building a better future, I have concluded that the best course for our people now is to formally surrender to the Ordeon Empire."

Angry shouts burst forth from the crowd, interrupting the chancellor and bringing a smile to Reno's face. Pride welled up within him at seeing his people's fierce determination to resist being conquered, despite all they had suffered.

When the crowd refused to obey the chancellor's pleas for silence, Canza gave a hand-signal and the mechs pointed the pulse guns at the end of their arms into the air and fired, shocking the crowd into silence.

"We have known nothing but war our entire lives. Nearly three generations of Vehlans and Ordonians have known nothing but war. It is time for us to know peace.

"I signed the surrender order last night, thus dissolving the Vehlan Union, its government, and its military. My last act as chancellor is to hand over all governing authority for Vehla and its territories to Emperor Johan Lentaise of the Ordeon Empire.

"It has been my honor to serve my people at the head of our government, but that honor now falls to the emperor. My wish is that you will cooperate with your new government and its leader in the best interest of both our people.

"Our goal was victory, but now it must be peace. I have faith you will strive for peace with the same zeal with which you fought for victory. Let us now rebuild."

Outdoor Stage
7:15 A.M.

The crowd was clearly unhappy with Macey's speech, and many glared at him with murderous rage as he finished and walked away from the gathering. When he was out of sight, they turned that hate towards Canza, but he suffered no fear or doubt as he replaced the chancellor at the podium.

He made a point of looking at General Reno in his disheveled blue uniform before he started speaking, drawing the crowd's attention to him and the four knights surrounding him.

The Star Knights was the organization responsible for the emperor's protection, not just for his physical person but for his interests as well. They were his eyes and ears across the empire and beyond, and when one saw them, they were to behave as if the emperor himself were present.

Their official reason for being here was to guard Reno, the last obstacle to the emperor's plans, but Canza knew the actual reason was to observe him. This caused him little concern, and he would do his job the same regardless of who was watching.

When sufficient time had passed for the Vehlans to recognize the predicament of their general, he turned to face them so he could finally put an end to the anarchy.

"The war is now over. We ended it yesterday by defeating the last of your military, and your chancellor prevented future bloodshed today by accepting that defeat. Two nations are now one, and we are now of the same people. There is no more cause for anyone to die," he spoke while carefully watching the faces of those listening.

There were a few who appeared willing to at least listen to what he had to say, but most continued to stare at him with expressions ranging from stubborn defiance to outright hate.

"We are ready to put all of this behind us and move on to build a better future, and as proof of this I am hereby extending an offer of amnesty to any former Union soldiers still at large who choose to turn themselves in. If you wish to continue serving your people, you may join the Imperial military where you will receive brief retraining, after which you will be allowed to retain your current rank and benefits.

"Should you choose to return to civilian life, you will be free to do so and will be left alone to live out the rest of your life in peace. This offer will be available for one week. Any who have not come forward in that time will be designated terrorists and subject to the full penalty of law."

This information appeared to soften some hearts as no doubt many were thinking of loved ones in military service they'd like to see return to a normal life.

At a subtle signal from Canza, the knights brought Reno forward to stand at the front of the stage.

"One such terrorist is with us here today, General Frederick Reno, commander-in-chief of the Vehlan Union Military. This war should have ended months ago, but blinded by pride, he prolonged it for as long as possible. His refusal to accept defeat led to the deaths of thousands on both sides.

"Despite this, I offered him one last chance to help us end the fighting and begin the rebuilding process. He still refused, and I am forced to declare him a traitor to the empire. There is only one punishment suitable for someone willing to create more death and destruction, only one way to guarantee they will no longer work against everyone's best interests."

Two of the knights grabbed Reno by the arms and forced him to stand on the stage edge where a box slightly larger than a coffin sat on the ground below.

"The lives lost because of him can never be replaced, but many more lives will be saved. Once he is gone, we will be able to build to far greater heights than either of our nations could have ever done on their own. A better future begins today."

The legion commander concluded his speech, then stepped away from the podium, signaling the knights to carry out the sentence.

Two doors on the top of the box slid open, and a white glow shone out to illuminate the look of sudden terror on the general's face. He struggled desperately against his guards, but they easily pushed him off the stage and into the box.

The doors slid closed again, but this did nothing to dampen the screams now coming from inside.

No one but the emperor and the knights knew what was in that box, but such knowledge was unnecessary for those present. Screams such as the ones they were now hearing were incentive enough not to commit any crimes meriting its use.

This continued for over a minute, then came sudden silence so thick a person felt unable to breathe.

All hints of defiance evaporated from the attendees as Canza waited for the demonstration's full effect to set in. There were some hushed whispers and he could hear someone crying, but most simply stood there.

Satisfied he had gotten his message across, Canza finally hand-signaled the soldiers around the crowd to disperse. These were imperial citizens now, and would be allowed to choose their own path.

Chapter Four
Forging On

Vehlan Escape Transports
10:01 A.M.

A soft-rustling sound broke the almost complete silence and drew Colonel Tyquese's attention towards the passenger section where he saw one of his soldiers making her way to the lavatory near the back of the craft.

He noticed a couple of the others looking at him as if waiting for something, but they quickly glanced away when his eyes connected with theirs.

Very little had been said since their narrow escape the day before as everyone knew there was nothing *to* say. The war was lost, their homes destroyed or in enemy hands, and there was nothing for them to do but hide and wait.

"Scout One, reporting in."

"Proceed, Scout One," Tyquese urged as he turned to face the instrument panel again while shifting his feet in an effort to work out some of the stiffness in his legs, wishing once again he was back on firm ground. There was never enough room on even the biggest of ships, and the vacuum of space was always one hull breach away from suffocating you.

The transports were maintaining an orbit above the last planet in the system which kept it between them and Vehla, effectively hiding them from the Ordonians but also preventing them from seeing anything that was happening. He needed to know what the imperials did next before he could make a move, so he'd sent a pair of soldiers in an escape pod to move close enough to Vehla to observe while still remaining unseen.

"We picked up an imperial broadcast from the planet, sir. Do you want me to send it to you on a private channel?"

"No. Relay it for everyone to hear."

Everyone learned at the same time of Chancellor Macey's formal surrender, the empire's offer of amnesty for all remaining union soldiers, and General Reno's barbaric execution.

Leon winced at the general's screams, but let the recording continue to play. This was the true face of the Ordeon Empire, and it would serve no purpose to hide it from his people.

Now they had something to talk about, and nervous whispers filled the cabin as the soldiers processed what they had just heard.

"What do we do now?" someone eventually asked loud enough for everyone to hear.

One soldier had the guts to say what they were all thinking, "There's nothing we can do. We have to go back and turn ourselves in. They promised we can live out the rest of our lives as we choose."

"Since when can we trust the empire to keep such promises?" Tyquese asked, his words creating instant silence.

He told the pilot sitting next to him to begin transmitting to all the ships, then he stood and turned to face the others. Some of them met his gaze, but the rest stared into empty space or held their heads in hands, one or two shaking from silent tears.

"Even if we can trust the Ordonians to allow us to live free after spending so much time fighting them, are we really willing to give up after all they have done?"

"What else can we do? We're not even soldiers anymore, and our nation is gone thanks to the chancellor."

"Which also means we don't have to do what you say!" another soldier insinuated.

A few murmurs of agreement worked their way through the group, but most appeared horrified anyone would ever suggest such a thing.

The colonel chose to pretend the last statement had never been uttered and continued making his case.

"I lost my sister when the Ordonians bombed Palcion as a 'distraction'. Both of my parents died in the nuclear attack on United. There is no way I can live my life in peace until justice is served on their murderers.

"Every Vehlan has suffered similar losses, including everyone here. Are you sure you're prepared to give up and forget about all of them?"

Silence fell, and the colonel looked each and every soldier in the eye while he awaited a response.

"How are we going to get that justice? Our entire military couldn't defeat them, so how are a mere handful of us in a bunch of transports supposed to do it?" someone asked.

"Macey did us a favor when he disbanded the military and dissolved the union. He made us into outcasts and renegades owing no allegiance to any nation with no obligation to conform to military rules and regulations, which I choose to believe is exactly what he intended."

This revelation shook a few more of them from their introspections and they looked at him with intrigue in their eyes as the implications began to dawn on them, but there was still some convincing to do.

"Aren't you making our point for us? We have no resources with which to fight," one soldier pointed out.

"Actually, I happen to know a rather powerful pirate captain with sympathies to our cause," Tyquese revealed with a secretive smile, and he finally saw understanding flicker in their eyes. Perhaps a spark of hope as well?

"We will have everything we need to return to the fight. All I need to know is that you are with me, that you will continue to fight and not give up! Remember that our voices are everlasting! Remember that we speak with the voices of the many, and the voices of the many cannot be silenced!" he concluded, hoping the quotes from the national anthem would encourage them and remind them why they fought.

Nothing happened at first, but then someone let out a cheer, another followed suit, and then another until everyone was cheering at the top of his or her lungs. Leon didn't cheer with them, but instead rose a fist towards the ceiling in a show of solidarity.

He looked back at the pilot, who reported that everyone in the other ships was also cheering, bringing a smile to his face as he found himself secure in the knowledge he could rely on them.

He gave one last shake of his fist for the soldiers, then returned to the co-pilot's seat and ordered their course to be set for Altaius.

No matter how long it took him, he would create a force strong enough to destroy the Ordeon Empire. There was no other purpose in his life now.

10:24 A.M.

The cheering finally subsided, and Eric opened his eyes to see everyone smiling and talking excitedly with one another.

He glanced towards the cockpit to see the pilot carefully working the controls in preparation for a hyperspace jump while the colonel sat beside him, staring at the main screen.

They had lost everything, but now they were supposed to follow a man on a quest for revenge poorly disguised as a pursuit of justice?

"Are you okay?" Jeremy questioned, interrupting his thoughts long enough to see that he was looking at him with obvious concern.

"I'm fine."

"Are you sure? Because it looks like you're about to puke."

“I said I'm fine!” Eric growled. His friend looked hurt and he was about to apologize but then Jeremy looked away and he chose to drop it instead.

How were they supposed to take on the entire Ordeon Empire when they didn't even have painkillers to get rid of the throbbing in his head?

Chapter Five
Behind Enemy Lines

Swarnlia
Monday, December 16th, 2607
9:27 P.M.

The deep dark created by the moonless night made it difficult to see amid the leafless trees, but Captain Helen Dodge maintained close watch nonetheless. She still had her ears, and the brush cover surrounding the cave entrance made it nearly impossible for someone to approach without making any sound even with the thick snow softening all noise.

A few strands of dark red hair drifted across her face and she deftly tucked them behind her left ear. Her hair was longer than regulations allowed, but she had given up trying to keep up with it months ago.

"It's freezing. We should start a fire," Sergeant Nate Caisen complained from his post on the other side of the cave to her right, his thick black beard revealing his own lack of military grooming habits. It helped that it also kept his face warm during these winter months which he enjoyed teasing her about.

"That would give away our position," she responded without losing focus for even a second.

"It's been over a year since we got stuck on this planet, and the Imps have never even come close to catching us. I doubt a little fire is going to help them find us now."

"We've evaded capture this long by being careful. They know we are here, and they have orbital control. Any anomalous heat signatures will raise suspicion."

"It's not like they can't detect our body heat."

"That's why we stay underground or under tree cover. A small fire inside the cave will never heat the rocks enough to be detected, but one out here will have the same effect as sending up a flare."

"They can't be watching the entire planet all the time. Besides, I say we let them come after us. Fanny and I can take care of 'em," the sergeant suggested, patting his large machine gun affectionately.

"You could do that, Gunney, but what happens if the Ordonians decide to just blast us from space?"

"That's where you come in, Dodger," Caisen teased, finally drawing a slight smile out of his superior.

It was a tradition in the Union Special Forces, the Azul Guardians, for each operative to be given a nickname by his or her peers. His love of big guns had gotten Caisen saddled with Gunney, while Dodge's was owed solely to her last name. It didn't stop the others from joking about her supposedly having a talent for dodging things, however.

"Sure, I could get out of the way, but what about the rest of you?"

"We'd manage," Gunney responded confidently.

The captain suddenly raised her right fist to call for silence, and a moment later they both heard muffled footsteps approaching their position. It sounded like a single individual, but they couldn't know that for sure.

They slowly raised their weapons to aim in the direction of the sound, then froze to make themselves invisible in the darkness.

The footsteps stopped, and Helen tightened her finger on the trigger as the silence deepened, ready to fire at the slightest provocation.

"Zero-Alpha-Sigma-Charlie," a voice spoke from the darkness.

"Approach," Dodge commanded, but kept her rifle ready. The code identified the speaker as Major Peter Briese, the leader of their team, but she wasn't taking any chances.

A shadowy form slowly stepped into view, and she switched on a small light attached to her rifle to see the major's stubbled face looking back at her. He was dirty and unkempt, but appeared uninjured and perfectly calm.

"Authenticated," she stated and finally lowered her rifle.

"What'd you find?" Gunney questioned.

"Inside. The whole team needs to hear this," Major Breise responded wearily, then walked past them and into the cave.

Three meters from the entrance the passage turned right, and the turn showed itself in flickering, orange light. Another two meters later they emerged into a small chamber where they found two men sitting near a fire in the center while a third lounged on a rock ledge in the shadows near a wall, all of them in various disheveled states.

"Exodus, take up watch outside," Dodge ordered one of the men by the fire.

When the empire invaded the planet, Private Exodus was cut off from his unit during the fighting and the team found him a few days later on the verge of collapse from hunger and exhaustion. Since he wasn't a Guardian he couldn't truly be considered a member of this team, so he was the only one who could step out to stand guard while the major briefed the rest.

"Yes, ma'am," the private responded, somewhat sullenly, then stood and picked up his rifle before heading towards the entrance.

"Are you wounded?" Specialist John Nafais, the team medic, asked the major from his position near the fire.

"No. Just tired and hungry."

A food pack came sailing through the air, and Breise caught it in both hands, then waved it towards Lieutenant Patrick Suese in a gesture of thanks before taking a seat on the ground by the fire.

"Our contact tells me that most of the population has settled down and accepted imperial rule or at least have chosen not to resist it, but there are still pockets of resistance like us. Ordonian efforts to eliminate us have proven ineffective, so they have decided to force us to surrender."

"We've been fighting them for over a year now without any backup and have still managed to inflict considerable damage. What makes them think we're going to give up now?" Gunney questioned.

"They are placing a nuke in every major city. They are threatening to detonate one per week unless all resistance ceases. The first one is to be in three days."

"You confirmed this?" Dodge asked.

"Yes. I infiltrated one of their camps and overheard soldiers discussing delivery of a warhead to Catania."

No one doubted the accuracy of this statement. The major's stealth skills were unrivaled, and he was described as being able to move as effortlessly as a light wind. This legend, along with the sound of his name, had earned him the nickname Breezy.

"We have to stop them," Nafais decreed.

"Security will be tight," Dodge commented. She didn't state this as a reason not to act, but merely as a realistic observation.

"Agreed on both counts, but I have an idea. One that will make the Ordonians think twice about using nukes, destroy one of their bases, and possibly increase our chances for rescue," Breise revealed.

"You had me at 'destroy one of their bases'," Gunney quipped.

"What's the idea?" Dodge wanted to know.

"We infiltrate Catania, steal that warhead, then smuggle it on their nearest base and detonate it once we've gotten away."

"How does that help our chances for rescue?"

"Vehla might not realize there are still soldiers trapped here, and we can't contact them, but an Ordonian base getting destroyed in a nuclear blast will send a clear signal that we are here."

"Who will be doing what?" Suese, the team sniper, asked.

"You and I will provide overwatch while Dodge, Caisen, and Nafais steal the nuke. Exodus will drive the escape vehicle."

"Let's do this," Dodge concluded.

Swarnlia
Catania
Wednesday, December 18th, 2707
3:03 A.M.

"I don't like this. We haven't seen a single civilian or enemy soldier," Captain Dodge whispered, her throat mic ensuring each member of the team heard her.

"Would you prefer to have to fight the entire way?" Nafais retorted from her left.

"Sure, why not?" Caisen joked from her right.

The captain found herself wishing their original mission had required armor with a helmet. Night vision and sound enhancements would be nice right now, but as it was, they had to creep through the city to maximize the utility of their natural senses.

"Catania was hit hard during the bombardment. Most of those who survived probably left to live with family or friends in less damaged areas, or they were evacuated by the empire," Major Briese suggested via comlink.

"That doesn't make any sense. Why would they threaten to nuke an empty city?" Dodge questioned.

"Don't forget that the Ordonians are as clever as they are cruel. Destroying an empty city shows their resolve, but preventing civilian casualties wins them points with the local population," Breise explained.

The ground team approached an intersection apparently undamaged during the invasion, and Dodge called for a halt by raising her right fist.

She signaled her teammates to take cover on either side of the street, then inched her way forward with rifle at the ready and swiveling from side to side.

A shot rang out, and she dove to her right, rolling into cover behind a truck.

"Target down," Suese reported.

Dodge was about to ask for details, but then glaring floodlights lit up the area and she was forced to shield her eyes or get blinded.

"Ambush! Fall back!" Briese exclaimed as plasma began raining down on the ground team.

"Eat laser, prissies!" Gunney screamed, stepping out of cover and letting loose with a spray of red laser bolts to cover Nafais as he ran back the way they had come.

He managed to take out a couple of the lights, allowing Dodge to pop up from behind the truck and provide him with cover fire while he fell back.

Several enemy soldiers entered the intersection, but three of them fell in quick succession to sniper fire, forcing the rest to jump into the nearest cover.

"We've got you covered! Fall back, Captain!" Briese ordered, so Dodge turned and ran after the others.

"Exodus, get to the secondary evac!"

"I can't! Enemy troops are at my position. If I move, they'll see me."

"Use your drone to create a distraction, then double-time it!" Breise insisted.

The ground team ran as fast as they could towards the subway tunnel that was their secondary evac route, firing behind them as they went. Dodge stayed at the six, ensuring no enemies got close, but the threat of sniper fire was enough to keep them at bay for now.

"Gunship!" Briese shouted, and the ground team instinctively ducked into the nearest doorway, but when she looked out and spotted the gunship, Dodge realized it wasn't after them.

"Get out of there!" she cried out just as the plane fired a pair of rockets at the sniper position.

They struck seconds later, lighting up the night with a powerful explosion, but there was no way to tell if the sniper team had gotten caught in it or not.

"Move!" she shouted and pushed the others back onto the street. The gunship pulled up, circled around and left the area, unable to come after the ground team due to the large buildings. However, without a sniper to worry about, the Ordonian foot soldiers began gaining ground.

They entered a small plaza and Dodge had just spotted the tunnel entrance when Caisen cried out in pain and went sprawling on to the ground.

The captain spun around, then dropped to one knee and opened fire on their pursuers while Nafais grabbed the sergeant by an arm and dragged him into cover behind an empty water fountain. Dodge tossed the last of her grenades, then joined them, almost shooting Private Exodus as he ran up to them.

"Anyone behind you?" she asked.

"Not that I can tell. I set the drone in their path and it was still firing by the time I was too far away to hear it."

"Yes or no would have been enough," she chastised, then ordered him to provide cover fire while she checked on Caisen.

"Lower back. Spinal damage. He can't walk," Nafais reported.

"Leave me here. I'll cover your escape."

"No. I'm not leaving you behind."

"Then you better tell Exodus to stop shooting so you can surrender, because that's your only other option."

She realized he was right, but however much she hated the idea of surrendering, she couldn't imagine leaving a man behind. Caisen must have seen the look on her face because he pulled his gun close and offered a weak smile.

"Fanny and I will buy you the time you need to get out of here."

"There's too many of them! We have to move!" Exodus shouted. Since there was nothing he could do for the sergeant, Nafais picked up his rifle and contributed to the cover fire.

Finally accepting there was nothing she could do, Helen squeezed her friend's shoulder, told him to go out in a blaze of glory, and gave the order for the others to move out.

"What about Breise and Suese?" Exodus wondered aloud.

"There's no way to know if they made it. Now move!" Dodge told him, then shoved him in the direction of the tunnel.

She followed and all three of them had made it inside the entrance when they heard the roar of Gunney's machine gun start up. The captain turned back to make sure no enemy soldiers were close, and spotted two people coming towards her from the right.

She took aim, but then the flashes of red light from Gunney's position lit them up and she realized it was Suese and Breise, the former practically dragging the latter at his side.

Ignoring the danger, she ran to them, put the major's free arm over her shoulders, and helped the lieutenant carry him to the tunnel.

"What happened?"

"He was hit in the head by flying debris," Suese answered. Dodge allowed Nafais to replace her in carrying the major, then set the explosives she had taken from Gunney on either side of the entrance.

"Goodbye," she whispered, and pressed the detonator.

Swarnlia

Catania

7:42 P.M.

On watch for enemy patrols and search teams, Captain Dodge perched beside a large window at the warehouse's front. It provided a clear view of the street, but was also dirty enough to partially conceal her, especially when she stayed in shadow.

They were unable to find a way out of the city after escaping the ambush, so they had holed up near the outskirts where Nafais could treat the major's injury while they waited for the heat to die down.

"He's coming around," the medic reported, and Dodge signaled Lieutenant Suese to take her place at the window. Nicknamed Scopes for his sharp eyes, he was the one she trusted most as a sentry next to herself.

"Report," Breise gasped when he saw her approaching.

"You were knocked unconscious by flying debris when a gunship fired rockets at your position. Lieutenant Suese managed to get you to the evac, but Sergeant Caisen was critically injured before reaching the tunnel. He volunteered to stay behind and cover our escape, allowing the rest of us to get away. I used the last of our explosives to collapse the tunnel entrance, preventing further pursuit. Sergeant Caisen is presumed KIA."

"There was no way to get him out?"

"No, sir. Any attempt to do so would have resulted in the death or capture of the entire team."

"What is the team's condition?"

"No major injuries, but we are out of explosives and almost out of ammo."

"We're also out of medical supplies," Nafais chimed in.

"Isn't there anything around here you can use?" Breise asked.

"Negative. Not much grows in a city."

His vast knowledge of the medicinal properties of plants had earned Specialist Nafais the nickname of Muddie. Such a quality was rare for a combat medic, but he enjoyed studying such things and took pride in the ability to live off the land.

"I need to speak to the captain in private," Breise stated, and everyone else respectfully moved outside hearing range, after which he told her that was their last chance to signal their people.

"We'll find another way, even if we have to seize an Ordonian comm. center," she insisted.

"We can't continue in our current condition."

"I disagree. We can steal or forage for anything we need. You said that there are other resistance cells out there, so we can always link up with them. All we have to do is hold out until our people can retake control of the planet."

"It's been over a year. Last we knew, the war was going badly for our side. If the union was capable of retaking the planet, it would have done so by now."

"That's why we have to keep striking at the occupation forces, to weaken them and give a counterattack the best possible chance of succeeding."

"We have no means of contacting our people, and Gunney is dead. If we continue like this, it won't be long before the rest of us join him."

"So what are we going to do? Surrender?" Dodge spat.

"No. Never surrender, but we do need to lay low for a while. We have to rest up, resupply, and most of all, we need information. There is only one place I can think of that meets all these needs," Breise responded, giving her a pointed look.

She looked at him in confusion, then recoiled in horror when she realized what he meant.

"No! I can't do that."

"We don't have a choice."

"I swore I would never go back."

"You also swore you would protect the members of this team."

"I won't do it," she stubbornly refused.

"Do you know of a better place?"

She didn't, but instead of admitting that, she just stared at him angrily.

"I'm not giving you a choice, Captain. I order you to take us to your family home."

She continued to stare at him, considering disobeying his order. He was looking for a safe place, but that was far from what she considered any location where her family was.

"Order confirmed," she finally responded.

The major gave her a sympathetic look, then asked how far it was.

"A few days using ground transportation."

"We'll need civvies to make it that far."

"Agreed," Dodge responded, then waved the rest of the team back over.

"Muddie, stay here and look after the major. Exodus, you're on lookout. Scopes, with me," she assigned duties, then led the way out the back of the warehouse.

One of these buildings had to have some clothes in it.

Chapter Six
Rewards

Ordeos
Friday, December 20th, 2707
11:32 A.M.

The empire's capital of Ordeos Prime appeared next to the sparkling blue water of the Eternity Ocean as the transport descended through the atmosphere, and Legion Commander Canza admired it from his position standing behind the pilot and co-pilot. The multitude of glass and solar panels reflected the sunlight to turn the city into a gleaming jewel, but all angles were carefully placed to prevent it from becoming blinding from any viewpoint.

It was a circular and fortified city surrounded by thick, reinforced stone walls, a unique feature not found anywhere else. This was partly symbolic to show the strength of the empire's resolve, but they were also fully functional to act as defensive barriers with advanced armor and weapon emplacements.

As the greatest engineering marvel in human history, the city served as the perfect example of the greatness of the Ordonian people and the prosperous future it promised all mankind.

They flew a victory lap around the city before landing, while citizens below packed the streets in the four outer districts, celebrating and cheering. Fireworks launched from the military and palace districts at the center, lighting the cockpit with periodic flashes of red, yellow, and green.

After they landed, Canza stepped up to the top of the ramp which descended from the back of the transport, and paused so he could bask in the light of the Ordonian sun. The light hurt his eyes after the dimness of Vehla and five days aboard ship traveling home, but he welcomed the pain. He was home.

When he looked down, he saw an honor guard lined up to form a path from the ramp to a limousine at the center of a convoy. He was glad, and felt honored, that the guard was made up of regular military personnel and not Star Knights.

"Legion Commander Max Canza and Legion Captain Tony Farra, I have been sent to escort you to an audience with the emperor," the guard captain stated when they reached the ground. Canza acknowledged him with a nod, then followed him to the convoy. The first and last vehicles in the procession were combat jeeps, the second and fourth were police SUVs, and the limousine was situated in the middle.

"Have you met the emperor before?" Farra asked after getting into the car.

"Once. He gave me command of the Vehlan offensive, then executed my predecessor. Now we see how he deals with success."

The convoy pulled onto the main road leading out of the spaceport, joining an even larger procession. Ten officers in full dress uniform, five in the black and red suits or dresses of the fleet and five in the red and green of the infantry, stood in a row behind a grand marshal, and behind them were two-hundred armored soldiers from a division which had participated in the final attack on Vehla.

Behind Canza's convoy were several tanks and combat jeeps, and that was as far as he could see, but he knew that emergency vehicles, parade floats, and marching bands would make up the rest of the procession.

They rolled out of the spaceport in perfect unison, entering the entertainment district as the first junction of a circuit of the entire city.

Citizens lined the streets, cheering and throwing confetti, but Canza and Farra kept their windows up as was tradition.

Next came the residential district, then the commercial district, after which they finally turned towards the city center where they entered the military district. All civilians stopped without entering, including those in the parade, and they were replaced by military personnel in dress uniform standing at attention with right fists on their hearts in the imperial salute.

They did a lap, then stopped in front of the single gate to the palace district at the exact center of the city. There was no vehicle access for this district, so they parked and got out where they encountered another honor guard, this time composed of Star Knights in their grey ceremonial robes with red and yellow trim.

No knight greeted them or saluted, but simply stood in silence on either side of the path leading to the palace itself. Canza and Farra also did not speak as they made their way down the path and up the twelve steps at the entrance where they were met by Master Knight Penavel, commander of the Star Knights.

He greeted them with a stiff nod, the best he could be bothered to give a non-knight, then led them inside, through the foyer, and into the throne room. The fifteen foot tall wooden doors already stood wide open, so they went straight in.

On each side of the throne room were fourteen gold columns with knights standing in the spaces between. A luxurious red carpet with five more knights on either side ran through the center of the room from the doors to the throne dais which sat at the top of ten steps. The emperor was pacing excitedly above the steps when they entered, but he stopped and stood still when he saw them. The empress was not present.

As they made their way down the carpet, the details of those on the dais became clearer. Four knights in ceremonial armor stood at each corner, acting as the emperor's personal guard. Their dark grey armor covered them completely, and they had rifles strapped to their backs with pistols holstered at their waists, but most notable were the swords also hanging from their waists as well as the tower shields they carried.

The swords and shields, which were a simple frame with an energy shield filling the center, were primarily ceremonial items, but the guards were trained to use them if necessary.

As for the emperor himself, he was clad in his royal robes, which were different shades of red save for the symbol of the Star Knights on his left breast and the seal of the emperors on his right. The crown sitting atop his black hair sported eight golden spikes with a large ruby at the base of each one and a smaller one at the top.

These trappings of his office accentuated his athletic frame and made him appear even taller than his already impressive height of two meters. He was unusually young for the position at thirty-one years of age, but he had already accomplished more during his reign than most of his predecessors, a fact which he made sure no one ever forgot.

"My emperor Johan Lentaise, I present to you the conqueror of Vehla, Legion Commander Max Canza, and his second-in-command, Legion Captain Tony Farra," Penavel announced upon reaching the throne, after which he gave a quick bow before taking his place at the bottom of the stairs to the emperor's right.

The officers put fist to heart in salute, bowed their heads, and got down on one knee.

"Welcome home, Heroes of the Empire! You will be remembered for all time for removing the last obstacle to our glorious future! Rise, and stand as proud men before me," the emperor proclaimed.

"You show us far too much honor, Majesty. The soldiers who died in battle are the true heroes," Canza remarked after standing up.

"They will also be remembered, but we're talking about you now," Lentaise reacted with some annoyance. Taking the hint, Canza chose to remain silent unless otherwise directed.

The emperor descended the throne stairs, stood in front of Canza, and placed his hands on his shoulders, all while smiling wide. Even standing on the same level, Lentaise still towered over the legion commander, the result of generations of genetic manipulation to ensure the royals always looked as regal as possible.

Canza was so surprised by this turn of events that he didn't even notice two of the personal guards take up position on either side of them. Emperors never took this level of familiarity with their subjects.

"Your victory over the Vehlans proved skills far beyond that of any Legion Commander. At last, someone is worthy to fill a position long empty, the duties of which I have been required to fulfill.

"Max Canza, I hereby promote you to the rank of Primary, commander of the entire Ordonian military and answerable only to me."

The revelation left Canza speechless, and the emperor's smile widened when he saw the effect of his words.

"You honor me more than words can say. I affirm my loyalty to you, the empire, and our ideals as a nation. I will perform my duties with efficiency, and will destroy all threats to our people."

He swore his oath, then remembered Farra was still standing next to him, and recalled the promise he had made.

"As my first act as Primary, and with your approval, I appoint Tony Farra as my secondary. He has proven himself worthy of my trust, and his loyalty to the empire is without question."

The emperor looked at Farra as if he was seeing him for the first time, and doubt clouded his features.

"I have never heard of him before. A secondary should have distinguished himself in some way to earn the position."

"He has distinguished himself to me, sire."

He still looked doubtful, but confirmed the promotion before returning to sit on his throne.

"Our first step is to prepare for our next campaign. There is no one who can challenge us now that the Vehlans are gone, but we still require substantial resources if we are to conquer all the nations," Lentaise broached the next subject.

"I agree, but the recovery process after a hundred years of war will be long and difficult."

"A powerful economy such as that in the Merchant's Interest would speed up that process considerably," Lentaise observed with a sly smile.

"Of course. As a protectorate of the union, the interest has no military of its own and can be annexed rather easily. There are also Vehlan military units hiding within their borders, which gives us cause to invade and prevents the other nations from allying against us until it is too late," Canza mused.

"Precisely. Once we have that economy at our disposal, we can support a military two or even three times larger than what we have now.""Agreed. I shall begin preparations immediately."

"No. Your secondary can do that. I have more to discuss with you," Lentaise dissented. Canza dismissed Farra with a nod, then turned back to the emperor who was smiling at him again.

"I have another reward for you."

"You have already honored me far beyond imagining. How could I accept any more?"

"You can accept it because I want to give it," Lentaise insisted, and Canza agreed with a nod.

"I name you governor of the Vehlan system. As it's conqueror, it is only right that you receive this privilege. Your word will be law."

His only response was to salute and bow respectfully.

"It will be your responsibility to integrate them into the empire, starting with taxes on all revenue totaling thirty-five percent and making our military in the sector self-sufficient."

"My emperor, I must object to paying taxes at this time. I recognize and accept your right to tax the provinces, but I request a reprieve of one year for Vehla. This way we can rebuild in a satisfactory amount of time," Canza protested.

"You speak your mind. A rare quality. Very well. No taxes will be collected from Vehla for one year. Do not disappoint me by failing to progress as expected."

"I understand, Majesty."

"There is a task I require of you today. I have rewarded you for your service, but now it is time for you to assist me in rewarding the people for their patience these long years."

"What did you have in mind?"

"The people love nothing more than a retired champion returning to fight in the arena. Today we will give them two champions!" the emperor revealed with a flourish. Canza had a feeling he knew where this was going, but he played along anyway.

"I relish the opportunity to return to the arena, but who would I be fighting?"

"Me, of course. We are both champions, and heroes for ending the war. It will be magnificent!"

Canza feared this was the man's idea, and considered rejecting the proposal. It was a risky proposition to fight the emperor, even in a simulated environment like the arena, but it was even riskier to turn him down.

"When do you want to do this?" he finally said, managing to fake a grin.

"Two hours. I'll make the announcement immediately so people can get to the arena. Prepare yourself, and meet me there."

Canza bowed, then exited the room.

He'd just been promoted to primary, and now he was preparing to fight the emperor in single combat. This was not how he had imagined his day was going to go.

Ordeos Prime Arena
1:53 P.M.

Thousands of people settled into their seats, filling the air with the dull roar of conversation while vendors walked the aisles and stairs between them. The youthful Empress Prailia Lentaise observed them from the royal box at center field while also keeping an eye on her two children in the box with her. The princes were young, but well-trained as befit their station, so they sat there with minimal fidgeting.

She had chosen to wear a sleeveless, dark red dress which sparkled when the light hit it, along with a diamond necklace and diamond bracelets. Her five-rubied silver crown sat atop her golden hair, carefully placed there to be held up by the hair alone without mussing it.

"Citizens of the Ordeon Empire, today is a most glorious day!" the announcement boomed out across the arena, and Prailia smiled when the crowd immediately quieted and looked toward the field excitedly. Surely the entire empire was silent at this moment as every citizen tuned in on their personal devices.

"One week ago today, the Vehlan Union was destroyed, along with any threat it posed. The menace which has stalled our development, and that of the entire human race, will be holding us back no longer!"

The crowd cheered at the top of its lungs, causing the youngest prince to wince slightly, but all three royals continued to sit quietly.

"This great victory could not have been achieved without the unwavering support of the Ordonian people. Our emperor wishes to commemorate the contributions of all citizens this day, starting with two champions returning to the arena to fight one another. Not only are they Arena Champions, they are also heroes of the empire!"

Another round of cheering ensued.

"Our first champion is the hero of the final campaign, the conqueror of Vehla, and our newly appointed primary, Max Canza!"

A gate on the north end of the arena slid into the ground, and the armored Canza marched out carrying a shield in his left hand while a shortsword swung at his side. Attendees cheered and clapped as he walked, but he did not acknowledge them.

When he reached the center, he pivoted on his right heel to face the royal box, put fist to heart in salute, then knelt on one knee with his head bowed while holding the salute.

"Our second champion is the hero of the war, the architect of the union's destruction, and our exalted emperor, Johan Lentaise!"

The south gate opened, and the emperor sauntered out, his open-faced helmet allowing everyone to see his broad smile. Two shortswords swung at his hips. Louder applause than before greeted him, and he happily waved at his subjects with his right hand as he walked.

He took up position a few feet to Canza's left and faced the box, acknowledging his family with a simple nod.

"Now, speaking for the emperor, I present our beautiful empress, Prailia Lentaise!"

All eyes turned to the royal box as Prailia stood and went to the front where everyone could see her. The stadium's jumbo monitors also displayed her image and amplified her voice.

"Five-hundred years ago, the human race was held tight by a chaos that threatened to swallow us whole, leaving nothing but silence in its wake. The severity of those struggles are still felt today as nearly all our history before that time was wiped out, as were the records of the chaotic times themselves. We do not even know for certain where our race originated.

"Then Haiden Lentaise emerged to restore order and establish an empire to prevent such a crisis from ever happening again. The generations that followed, including our own, have desired nothing more than to better themselves and bring peace and prosperity to all people," she began her speech.

She paused to gauge the crowd. They were listening intently, but gave no reaction. This was nothing they hadn't heard before.

"However, a group of malcontent nations banded together to oppose us, calling themselves the Vehlan Union. They eventually dropped the pretense of a coalition and consolidated into a single nation, one full of corruption and greed. Ever since that time, they have opposed us, hampering our efforts to advance the human race."

Murmurs of displeasure rippled through the crowd, but quickly dissipated. A child cried out, then was silent again.

"We ignored them at first, leaving them to their opinions while we worked elsewhere. Mutual tolerance wasn't good enough for them, however; and they attacked us every time we made progress with other nations, forcing us to withdraw our aid to those people. We attempted a diplomatic solution, but they insisted the only possibility for peace was for us to join their union and adopt their backwards ways."

Whispers of discontent and disbelief passed around the stands, and she waited patiently for them to die down. Johan smiled proudly at her from the field below, but Canza had yet to move from his bowing position.

"One-hundred years ago, our patience ran out, and Emperor Lukin Lentaise attacked the union, vowing never to stop until it was destroyed, and the path forward made clear. Unfortunately, he underestimated the enemy's strength, and he did not live to see his vow fulfilled. His son, Calin Lentaise, carried on in his name, but fell in battle before he could finish, adding his heroic sacrifice to millions of others."

She put her right hand over her heart and bowed her head, signaling a moment of silence for the fallen. Nothing stirred, not even a breeze, as they remembered all those who had fought and died for the promise of a better future.

Returning to her previous stance, she continued the speech.

"Four years ago, Johan Lentaise ascended the throne, shouldering the responsibility of finishing a war which had already lasted far too long. He realized the need for new, unconventional tactics, and promptly instituted them. Stuck in its ways, the union was unable to face us on these new terms, and rapidly fell to our advance. Now they are destroyed, and we stand strong."

There was a quick cheer and a round of applause, but she raised her hands to call for silence.

"This triumph was made possible by the sacrifices of the Ordonian people over the course of this last century. We honor the lives lost fighting this evil, but we also commend all those who labored tirelessly to keep the empire strong all these long years.

"Today, we reward each and every imperial citizen with celebrations lasting all day. We welcomed our heroes back home with a magnificent parade, and now we give you an arena match between two great warriors that have proved themselves in the arena and battle. Our heroes, Emperor Johan Lentaise and Primary Max Canza!" she finished with a wave of her arm towards the contestants, and the crowd shot to its feet to deliver a standing ovation full of shouting and screaming.

On her last word, Canza finally stood up, then drew his sword in succession with the emperor, and both of them raised their weapons towards her in a warrior's salute. She acknowledged them with a wave, then sat down again, at which point she noticed her youngest son had begun to fidget. She shot him a disapproving look, and he stilled himself.

2:11 P.M.

The empress's speech was a good one, but Max was glad it was over. His joints were getting stiff from bowing for so long.

After saluting the royal family, the combatants turned to face each other, then saluted again with their weapons before taking ten steps back.

There was little real danger in arena matches thanks to a combination of stun weapons and injury simulating suits, but there was little that could be done to prevent actual injury from certain attacks, such as having a shield plow into your side.

The suits worked by registering where a weapon struck, calculating the damage it should do, and numbing body parts accordingly. Even blood loss was simulated by slowly weakening the wearer, and a killing blow resulted in unconsciousness.

Combatants were trained to pull their punches, swinging just hard enough to register a hit but stopping short of causing harm, but there was no way to eliminate such things completely.

The start buzzer sounded, and Lentaise charged forward as the crowd erupted in cheers. He advanced quickly and raised both swords high to the right, but Canza held his ground to the last second, then dodged to the left, causing his opponent to go past him.

Lentaise reacted by spinning to his right and swinging his swords around, but Canza got his shield up in time to block them. The force of the blow was so strong that it still managed to knock him off-balance, forcing him to take a couple steps back.

The emperor exploited this by hitting the shield again with his right sword while bringing the other down towards Max's shoulder, but he managed to block the move with his own sword. He then used his shield to push him back, then thrust his sword towards his gut, but Lentaise jumped back before it could connect.

His blitz attack having failed, the emperor moved farther away and began circling.

"You are a worthy opponent," he commented.

"As are you," Canza responded.

They continued to circle, studying each other and watching for the tiniest opening that would grant them an advantage.

This lasted for about a minute with no opportunities presenting themselves, and Canza decided it was time to move things along. In an actual fight, he would have waited for as long as it took to spot a weakness, but this was a game, and a lack of action made for poor entertainment.

He loosened his left arm and let his shield drop slightly, expecting the emperor to sweep it away from the inside, but instead he hit it full-force with both swords. The loose arm was unable to absorb the attack, and he was knocked to the ground.

The emperor stepped on his right wrist, disabling his sword hand, and brought both swords up to stab down in an elaborate finishing move.

This left his torso open, allowing Canza to bring his shield around and slam it into his ribs, knocking him to the ground and giving him time to jump back onto his feet.

2:32 P.M.

The emperor swung a sword towards Canza's ankles, forcing him back long enough for him to stand up again. He resisted grabbing his side as pain shot through his body, and gripped his swords tight as they squared off again.

Canza came at the emperor shield first, who was forced to use both his swords to block and keep from being run over, but Canza had his sword positioned to come up under them and into his chest.

Lentaise countered by stepping to the side and releasing his block, causing his opponent to stumble forward under his own momentum. Before he could recover, the emperor slashed a sword across his back, and the primary cried out in pain and frustration.

The emperor moved in to press the attack, but Canza swung at his face, forcing him back.

Once again, they settled in to circle around each other. The more they fought, the more they came to recognize the ability of the other, causing them to realize great care was needed if they were to stave off defeat.

The royal box came into view, and Lentaise spotted Prailia watching them intently. Was that concern he saw in her eyes?He considered her a friend, but their marriage was one of political convenience, not love. She was the daughter of a governor of a province world that had been ignored by the central government due to the war with the union, along with many others. As crown prince, he had gone out to those worlds and seen to their needs.

When he met her at a banquet thrown in his honor by her father, they had easily engaged in conversation. He married her shortly afterwards, then left the continuing work in the region to her while he returned to more important duties.

Did she really care enough about him to have concern for his safety in a mock battle?

The question left his mind as quickly as it entered, and he focused entirely on the fight.

His opponent offered no opening, but he attacked anyway, charging into him and raining down a series of rapid blows. Canza blocked each one until he was finally forced to retreat or risk exhausting himself.

3:16 P.M.

The two contestants faced each other in the arena's center, having fought around the entire field and returned to the start. They stood there, breathing heavily, grasping one sword in both hands, and doing their best to ignore their many injuries. Canza looked into the emperor's eyes, and finally saw what he had been waiting for.

Lentaise took a deep breath, then jumped at him, bringing his sword from high to low with all his remaining strength. Canza blocked by putting his own sword above his head, but the sheer force of the attack still knocked him onto his back.

Unable to pull back, the emperor tripped over him and sprawled into the dirt on the other side, where he stayed without moving.

"Unbelievable! Neither combatant can continue! The match is a draw!" the announcer proclaimed.

Arena aides rushed in and helped them to their feet, then deactivated the suits to remove the numbing effects. The numbed areas came alive with the sensation of pins and needles, which was quickly replaced by the dull ache of muscle fatigue.

Once they were sure there were no serious injuries, the aides stepped back, the opponents stepped up to each other and each held his sword across his own chest, officially signaling a draw. The two of them then walked off the field together as workers flooded the field to prepare it for the next event, a re-creation of the last battle to take the Vehlan fortress.

"You did well, and have proven yourself worthy of being my primary," Lentaise commented.

"Did you have doubts?"

"The only way to truly know someone is to fight them. Today you demonstrated your ability, and your resolve."

"I will not fail you, Majesty."

"I will hold you to that," Lentaise warned as they passed through the south gate. He changed the subject as they made their way to the preparation rooms.

"I had a book delivered to your home here in the city. It is a book known only to the emperor and whomever he deems worthy, and it contains a history lost to all others. With the union gone, we will have more time and resources to put the information it contains to good use."

"I will read it as soon as possible, but my first priority should be to join Farra in preparing for the invasion of the Merchant's Interest."

"Agreed. Join me in the palace's tactical center after you have cleaned up."

3:59 P.M.

Satisfied that all was in order, a freshly showered Primary Canza in dress uniform exited the preparation rooms to find an older couple waiting for him outside.

"Mother. Father. I was not expecting you," he admitted as they drew closer.

"We came to see your fight," Rita, his mother, responded.

"Our son, the Conqueror of Vehla, and the emperor's new primary. How could we not come see you?" Heath, added.

"Is there something you need to tell me?"

"No, we just wanted to see you," Rita assured him.

"We were wondering what you're going to do now."

"The first thing to do is to capture any union soldiers that have not turned themselves in and screen prisoners of war for potential release. We also need to incorporate Vehla and its territories into the empire. That is all I can say at this time."

"It was generous of the emperor to grant amnesty to surrendering soldiers, but he's also granting the Vehlans citizenship? I'm not sure how I feel about that," Heath remarked.

"I agree. It would be better for everyone if we made them slaves like we did with the Nosines," Rita concurred.

"The war is over. It is time for us to move on. The Vehlans were blind to this fact, but our actions were always meant to benefit them as much as ourselves. As governor of Vehla, I intend to see to it that all those under my authority receive equal rights."

"They haven't earned those rights," Heath refuted.

"They will. I'll see to it."

"They will never measure up to the rest of us. In the end, they will always be Nihls," Rita insisted.

"I have a lot of work to do," Max stated, tiring of the conversation.

"Of course. The Vehlans were only the beginning, and I'm sure you're eager to deal with the rest of our enemies," Heath responded.

There was nothing more to say, so Max simply walked away, turning a deaf ear to his parents telling everyone within earshot that he was their son.

Chapter Seven
A New Start

Altaius
Saturday, December 21st, 2707
11:03 A.M.

"Establish a perimeter," Colonel Tyquese ordered as soon as the ships touched down.

The troops jogged off the ship, and the colonel followed shortly afterwards, blinking his eyes in the sudden brightness. Genetic alterations received by all soldiers native to Vehla allowed their eyes to quickly adjust to the light from different suns, and he had set the lighting aboard the ships to match that of the Altaiun sun, but it still took some time for his eyes to acclimate to the brightness of the desert.

When he could finally see properly, he descended the ramp and observed the soldiers as they created a defensive line around the ships. Their stiff movements spoke to the cramped quarters they'd endured for the last eight days, traveling in ships designed for trips of mere hours.

In ships meant for long journeys, it normally took less than two days to travel the forty-three lightyears from Vehla to Altaius. The escape craft from Blue Fire Fortress were not such vessels, requiring them to fly at slower speeds to conserve fuel, and they still had to stop to resupply twice. Fortunately, Leon still knew of a few places safe from the empire.

Whatever the trials, they had made it, and he was glad to be on solid ground once more.

"Perimeter set, Colonel," Captain Mathison reported. He was the highest ranked officer next to Leon to escape the base, which made him the default second-in-command.

"I'm headed out to speak with the pirate captain. Assemble four soldiers to go with me. If they still have rifles, take them. They are to be equipped with pistols only. You're in command while I'm gone."

"I should be the one to go, sir."

"I appreciate your concern, Captain, but I have to be the one to go. If the pirates see soldiers they don't recognize, they'll shoot first and ask questions later. Their captain is an old acquaintance of mine, so once he sees me, he will know we mean no harm and we'll be safe."

The captain nodded, then gathered the colonel's escort. One of the soldiers resisted giving up his rifle at first, but then consented when he saw the disapproving looks of his peers. Some commanders might have seen his actions and doubted his loyalty , but Leon chose to overlook the infraction for now. They had all been through a lot, and any strictness from him would only fray their nerves further.

He made sure everyone knew not to make any hostile moves, then set out on foot. It would take a couple hours this way, but it was a less aggressive approach than a fast-moving ship and he needed to stretch his legs anyway.

He only hoped that he was right about the pirate captain not wanting to hurt him.

1:33 P.M.

An insect buzzed around Eric's face, and he forcefully brushed it away. When it came back, he clapped his hands on it, the resulting sound seeming thin in the open, rocky desert.

He wiped the remains on his pants, ignoring the snobbish sneers of the others in the colonel's party, the colonel himself appearing not to notice the disrespect for the armor. The private was seriously considering defecting at this point, so he really didn't care what any of them thought.

Would it truly be defecting, anyway? The union government was gone, so who was going to charge him with the crime? He could go his own way, find someplace far from the empire and make a new life for himself, perhaps even finding a little happiness. That certainly sounded a lot better than trudging through a desert for over two hours under a sun intent on burning his face off, following a man he wasn't entirely convinced was still sane.

The argument was purely academic at this point, however. He was stuck on a planet full of homicidal criminals, and the only ships he could use were being guarded by thousands of his fellow soldiers.

His only hope of getting away would be by convincing some of the others to go with him, but that wasn't going to happen with the colonel around, so for now he just kept his thoughts to himself.

The group crested a hill and paused when they saw a crude paramilitary complex a couple miles in front of them. Walls made from a variety of materials surrounded the base, but they looked too weak to do anything other than simply slow down an attacking force. There were guard towers of similar construction at regular intervals on the inside of the wall, and further in he could see several buildings that looked as if they were about to fall down.

These were the ones meant to help them defeat the Imps?

2:01 P.M.

As he approached the gate to the pirate base, Leon spread his arms wide to indicate peaceful intentions. The guards at the top aimed rifles at them, but held their fire. A good sign.

He stopped a few yards from the gate and his soldiers took up position on either side of him, hands hovering near their holsters.

The gate opened and the pirate captain walked out, flanked by four guards of his own. His dark skin revealed him to be a Vehlan, but that meant little in these circumstances.

Leon immediately noticed that all five pirates were also equipped with pistols only, another good sign, and relaxed enough to drop his arms.

"I never expected to see you again," the pirate captain stated.

"You should have known better."

"I figured you were too busy with your little war to even pay attention to where I was."

"No matter how busy I get, I always make time for the important things."

"So I'm important to you now?"

"You always were. We've disagreed on many things, but that doesn't change who we are to one another."

"I've never known who I was to you."

"You are someone about whom I care a great deal."

"Apparently you didn't care enough to make yourself presentable."

"When you're running for your life, there isn't a lot of time to stop for a shower or change of clothes," Leon retorted.

The captain studied him as if unsure whether to believe him, or if he wanted to believe him, but he eventually ordered the gate guards to lower their weapons and dismissed his entourage with a wave of his hand.

"Well, you came all this way. The least I can do is hear what you came to say. You and your soldiers are under my protection while we are talking," he announced.

The pirates looked confused, glancing between their captain and Leon, but then they just shrugged and walked away.

"Private Olian, contact Captain Mathison and inform him we have arrived and our safety has been guaranteed for the time being," Leon ordered, then followed the captain into the base.

"So what brings my older brother all the way out to the middle of nowhere to consort with criminals," the captain asked. The soldiers glanced at their colonel in surprise, but said nothing.

"We need your help," Leon admitted, causing his little brother to stop in his tracks and stare.

"You need *my* help?"

Leon's only response was a short nod.

The captain noticed the soldiers as they kept looking between the two of them, likely looking for familial similarities.

"Yes, I am Sam Tyquese, known to the pirates as Red Sam and captain of a pirate faction, younger brother of the colonel here, and traitor to the union," he snapped, and the soldiers quickly looked away.

Leon opened his mouth to say something about not taking things out on them, but stopped himself.

"It would be best to continue our talk in private," he said instead.

They spent the rest of their trek through the base in silence, eventually coming to a command center. The first thing Leon noticed upon entering was the color theme. Different shades of red adorned every surface, including the elevator they rode up to the fourth floor.

They exited the elevator into what looked like the waiting room for a psychiatrist's office. It was set up for comfort with two small couches and six upholstered chairs around a couple tables with lamps and reading material. Once again, everything was a shade of red.

Of course, not many doctor's offices had guards next to the elevator and the door to the office itself.

“Your men can wait here,” Sam stated, then entered the office without waiting for a reply. Leon nodded at the soldiers, signaling them to do as the captain had instructed, then followed his brother.

“Alright, I have to ask. What is with all the red?”

Sam was already seated behind a red metal desk, in front of which were two red leather chairs. The walls and carpet were red, as were the lamps and other furniture scattered around the room.

“Tradition. Pirate factions are designated by color, which is determined by personality and abilities. My faction is known for strong military tactics, but is also fair and reasonable, and apparently red is the color which most accurately reflects those things.”

“I thought you didn’t care about such things, and would have decorated however you wanted,” Leon commented as he took a seat in front of the desk.

“I worked hard to earn the loyalty of my pirates, and I'm not about to do anything to compromise that,” Sam asserted, and Leon nodded his understanding.

“I heard the union was finally defeated. I figured you were dead, since I knew that was the only way you would ever let that happen,” Sam broached the next subject.

“Then the fact that I am still alive should tell you the union is not yet defeated,” Leon argued. Sam sighed and leaned further back into his chair.

“Give up, Leon! The union died long before the empire fired the last shot, which is why I left. It sacrificed too many of its principles, and its people, in its great crusade until it became nothing more than a facade.”

Leon let out a defeated sigh and leaned forward to hang his head, “You tried to tell me, but I didn't see it back then. I believed in our cause and thought you were overreacting to necessary steps towards victory. By the time I realized you were right, it was too late for me or anyone else to do anything about it. Not while the empire was holding a knife to our throat.”

Past defeats and failures weighed heavy on him, but then he remembered his life's purpose and shot out of his chair. He walked around to its back and leaned on it to punctuate his next point.

"We lost our way, and the war, but I still believe in our cause. Things are different now, and there is still hope. We have the chance to rebuild the union, to make it what it was always meant to be."

"You're being too idealistic, as always. Even if we managed to rebuild the union, it would all happen again. Decades or centuries from now, it will all fall apart. We're better off finding our own way."

"We can't let that stop us. We have to try to do better, or else there is no point in living."

"Then I suggest you find a new point to life."

Frustration rose within him like boiling water, but Leon resisted the urge to lash out and continued illustrating his point.

"Separate from all of that is the fact the Ordonians still need to face justice for all the crimes they have committed. Because of them, you and I are all that remains of our family, and hundreds of millions of others have died at their hands. The union was all that stood in their way — so many more are going to die if we don't act."

2:22 P.M.

The room fell silent as Sam considered his brother's words. He wanted nothing to do with the union, or his brother for that matter, and he wasn't interested in helping the latter rebuild the former. However, he couldn't deny there was a part of him that wanted to strike out at the Imps and make them pay for all they had done.

As thoughts of the past pulled him deep inside himself, his gaze drifted to a picture of his sister on his desk. She was dressed in a bright white uniform with two blue vertical stripes on the front, smiling wide at the chance to finally serve in the war as a nurse helping people near the front lines. She was the only one in the family who had ever understood him, the only one he knew he could trust without reservation.

"You speak of the empire needing to be brought to justice, but it is not responsible for the deaths in our family. It was the union's responsibility to protect them, and it failed. It has suffered the penalty for its negligence," he finally spoke up.

Leon followed his gaze to the picture, then picked it up to take a closer look.

"She was the only connection between you and me, the only one who could get us to get along, or at least tolerate each other. That's up to us now," he mused, then set the picture back down.

He reached into his jacket, pulled a folded photo from an inside pocket, and propped it up against the frame of Kate's picture, facing Sam. This one was taken at the same time as Sam's but featured the entire family. Their parents were standing behind the three of them, and Kate stood in the middle with an arm around each brother.

The older brother kept his eyes on the pictures as he declared, "She believed in helping people, and that was exactly what she was doing when the empire attacked by bombing lightly defended civilian targets from space. Our parents were at home, minding their own business, when an Ordonian nuke vaporized them. The union did not kill them, the empire did."

"Right now, it really doesn't matter who killed them. I'm a pirate now, and serving justice isn't high on my list of priorities. The one thing I do care about is making a profit. A resistance movement carries with it a lot of cost, but I don't see any profits," Sam refuted.

At this, Leon sat down again and leaned forward as if he was about to tell the greatest secret in the universe.

"Both of us stand to gain a great deal from such an alliance. Now that the union is gone, the empire is indisputably the most powerful nation in the galaxy, and also the richest. As I said before, with no one to stop them, they will begin moving on to the other nations, which means a lot of supplies moving around. You and the other pirates will be increasing your raids against them soon, regardless of whether or not we work together.

"My people and I know how the empire operates, and we can use that knowledge to help you raid its supply lines and get out with minimal loss and maximum profit."

"I'm not the only Vehlan deserter among the pirates. We fought them as soldiers, and we've fought them as pirates. There are also many Ordonian deserters among our ranks who brought with them knowledge and experience that goes far deeper than your own. How does anything you bring provide any added benefit?"

"All of those people, including yourself, have seen only small pieces of a grander scheme. As General Reno's adjutant, I saw it all. There is little any of us can do to improve your odds in individual battles, but I can create an overall strategy which will guarantee maximum gains."

This was starting to sound like something Sam could get behind, but he would still have to show those under his command something more substantial up front if they were going to go along with it.

"How many soldiers are with you?" he asked.

"Nearly two-thousand."

Sam practically jumped out of his chair and began pacing behind his desk. Leon watched him with a quizzical expression, but said nothing as his brother mulled things over.

He hadn't expected it to be so many, but now he could see a lot more potential to the proposed alliance, in particular the chance to eliminate a persistent nuisance. One strategy after another rapidly played out in his mind as he paced until he finally settled on one.

The pirate spun on one heel behind his chair and looked into his brother's eyes.

"I'm prepared to work with you, but there's something you have to do for me before anything else."

"What would that be?"

"Thanks to my efforts, the red faction is now one of the most powerful factions. There is actually only one other captain with enough power to threaten us: a woman named Black Tempest."

"A woman? I've never heard of a female pirate captain before," Leon commented.

"It's rare, but it does happen. Tempest managed it by killing the previous captain during sex."

"Dare I ask what black means in your system?"

"No other faction would follow a captain that would kill someone in such a way. That alone should tell you enough," Sam explained. The look of concern already on Leon's face deepened, but he told his brother to continue.

"Once we combine our forces, no faction will be strong enough to resist us, not even Tempest. We launch a surprise attack, eliminate her, and I take her resources for my own. Then none of the others will be able to stand against me, even if they band together, and I can use that to force them to submit to my authority. I get ease of mind knowing my position is secure, and you get an even stronger beginning to your resistance force."

"I'd hardly call that a strong beginning. How can we know the other captains and their followers can be trusted?"

"Let me worry about that."

"This will never work if we have to spend all our time worrying about someone stabbing us in the back. I need to know they can be trusted," Leon insisted, reminding Sam of how his older brother had never believed in him.

"I wouldn't be alive right now if I didn't know how to deal with the other pirates and their captains. I said I will handle it, and that's what I'll do," he stated, his tone hardening.

Silence fell as the two stared at each other and Leon considered his options. Then he finally stood and reached across the desk.

“I agree,” he said. Sam glared at the offered hand, then hesitantly took it in his own to shake hands.

“There's something else we need to take care of first,” Leon mentioned.

“What?” Sam responded, eyes narrowing suspiciously.

“The Ordonians know enough of us escaped to be a potential threat. They'll hunt us down unless we give them a reason not to.”

It only took a moment before a coy smile spread across Sam's face.

“I recently heard about some lightly armed transports fleeing the Ordonian blockade of Vehla. My source tells me they are full of soldiers, which also means there's plenty of valuable military equipment aboard. A prime target for a pirate, but the soldiers will resist and most will die in the raid. Rotten luck after escaping an invasion, but such is life.”

Leon nodded his understanding and turned to leave, but Sam still had one more thing to say.

“Oh, and get rid of the flag on your armor and tell your people to do the same. You're not soldiers anymore.”

Vehlan Base Camp
6:12 P.M.

“This is pointless!” Eric exclaimed as he dropped his crate outside the transport.

“We have to take the supplies off the ship so it can be used if needed,” Jeremy responded, and carefully set his own crate down. Eric couldn't tell if that's what he actually thought he meant, or if he was being deliberately dense.

“I'm talking about taking orders from a colonel determined to fight an unwinnable war.”

“Oh. Well, he still holds out hope.”

"Then he's an idiot."

"Alright then, what do you suggest we do?"

Afraid someone might overhear, Eric stepped closer to his friend and spoke in low tones.

"I say we take one of those ships and get out of here while we can. We can go to the Merchant's Interest and start over away from all this insanity."

"What happens when the Imps conquer the interest? If they ever discovered where we come from, they'd arrest and probably execute us. Would we just move on to another nation, then another, and another?"

"What are you talking about?"

"The Ordeon Empire has never been shy about letting people know it intends to conquer everyone. Now that the union is gone, there is no one to stop them from doing exactly that. Somebody has to stand against them, and it might as well be us."

"If nations have no hope of standing against the empire, then what can we possibly do? I'd rather try to make a life for myself than die fighting for a lost cause."

"Sure, you might continue breathing, but only by abandoning your principles. Doesn't sound like much of a life to me."

"Principles such as bringing criminals to justice? Criminals like the ones we just allied ourselves with?"

"We need allies to do any good, not to mention stay alive. This argument is what's pointless. We swore oaths as soldiers to uphold the ideals of the union and defend its people."

"Both of us were drafted and essentially forced to make those oaths, which in my opinion means they're not truly binding. Besides, the union doesn't exist anymore, freeing everyone from their obligations. Isn't that what the colonel said makes it okay for us to work with pirates in the first place?"

The two of them stared at each other, and Eric thought he had finally convinced Jeremy to go with him, but he should have known better.

"Fine. If you want to desert, go ahead. I'm going to stay right here and keep fighting. Even if there isn't any hope, I'd rather die fighting than live in fear," Jeremy snapped at him, then grabbed his crate and walked off.

Eric looked after him, then glanced at the transport and considered just taking it and fleeing by himself, but then he sighed and picked up his crate before following his friend.

There really wasn't anything else he could do.

Chapter Eight
No More Union

OES Dragon's Breath
Monday, December 30th, 2707
1:23 P.M.

The digital desktop displayed a multitude of reports from Vehla, and Canza carefully pored over each one. Farra was taking care of the preparations for the new campaign, so he had decided to return to the planet in his new role as governor to oversee the beginning phases of the reconstruction.

He was pleasantly surprised to see that the native population was offering no resistance, and many were even volunteering to help. Had they finally grown tired of conflict after all?

Another report showed a few small gaps in their security measures, and he promptly outlined new protocols and transmitted them. It didn't matter how much the Vehlans were cooperating, he wasn't about to let down his guard.

"Primary Canza to the bridge! Urgent!"

He deactivated the screen and rushed out the door and onto the bridge.

"Report!"

"We picked up a distress call from ships identifying themselves as Vehlan military. I have ordered an intercept course — best speed," the captain explained after vacating his chair for the primary to take.

"What's the nature of their distress?"

"Pirates. They claim to be lightly armed transports. I believe they are the ones that escaped from Vehla, sir."

"Why?"

"All other enemy troops have gone to ground, and wouldn't expose themselves like this. What I don't understand is why they are headed for Ordonian space. It makes more sense for them to go to the Merchant's Interest."

"They're out for revenge. They have nothing left to lose, so they decided to become terrorists," Canza concluded.

"Approaching distress call origin," Helm reported.

"Drop to normal space. Condition Red."

The milky whiteness of hyperspace disappeared to be replaced by star-studded blackness, and the interior lighting dimmed as the ship entered combat mode. Half of the main screen switched to a tactical view, but it showed no other ships in the area, only debris.

"Tactical, are you registering any possible threats?" Canza queried.

"Negative, sir."

"Operations, report."

"The materials and energy signatures confirm the debris comes from ships that were the same type and number of the transports that escaped Vehla, sir. I'm also detecting enough biomass to indicate over one-thousand casualties."

"There was enough room on those ships for three-thousand," the captain interjected.

"Nearly two-thousand are confirmed to have escaped," Canza added.

"Then what happened to the rest of them?"

"They likely saved themselves by joining the pirates."

"It hasn't been that long. We can still give chase, sir," the captain responded, alarm creeping into his voice.

"No, that won't be necessary. They are no longer a threat. The pirates are nothing but a nuisance, and we'll deal with the remaining Vehlans in the Merchant's Interest soon enough. Resume course to Vehla."

There was nothing left to stand between the empire and it's destiny.

Swarnlia
3:06 P.M.

The truck bumped along to a stop on the side of the road, and Helen stepped out to approach the car following her. Her passenger, Lieutenant Suese, joined her.

"Is there a problem?" Major Briese asked from the driver's seat. As his wounds healed, he'd insisted on helping with the driving. The team had started out traveling together in a single van, but switched to two vehicles as soon as they could to avoid suspicion. Since he was also a native of the planet, Private Exodus stayed with the second group to act as a guide should they get split up.

"We're almost there, but I think it's best if I go on ahead to explain the situation," Helen explained.

"Negative. None of us can afford to be going off on our own right now."

"I'm not in any danger here. Nobody around here is capable of hurting me even if they wanted to."

"And the Ordonians?"

"It's a small farming town, Major. Even if the empire has a presence here, it will be small and easy to avoid."

The major thought about it, clearly hesitant to put any member of his team at even the slightest risk, but he finally agreed to let her go alone.

"There's a bar about a mile up the road. Wait for me there."

Twenty minutes later she was rolling down the driveway to her family's farm, still trying to figure out what she was going to say. She hadn't spoken to her father or any of her siblings since she joined the army against their wishes.

She parked the truck, strode up to the door and knocked loudly, her heartbeat quickening in her chest. Somehow she was more afraid about the impending conversation than when she was about to go into battle.

The door opened to reveal her father Reuben, looking the same as when she'd last seen him except for the gray which had replaced his brown hair. Tall and strong, he stared at her with the stern expression he always wore around her.

"You're still alive," he commented.

"My stubbornness came in useful for something," she joked, hoping to relieve the tension.

She failed.

"Why are you here?"

"It wasn't my choice."

"Since when do you do anything against your will?"

"Since my superior officer gave me an order. My team needs a safe place to hide for a while."

"You know I want nothing to do with the military."

"And you know I wouldn't be here unless it was absolutely necessary. If we don't find a safe haven, we'll probably be dead within a month," Helen argued. If this lasted much longer, she'd walk away, orders or no orders.

Her father stared at her some more, then looked her up and down and finally seemed to relax.

"When was the last time you bathed?" he quipped, wrinkling his nose. She was tempted to respond to his joke the same way he had to hers, but decided she was too tired for banter.

"Year or so ago," she replied.

"That must mean you're the ones who've been resisting the occupation."

"We're not the only ones."

"Actually, you are. The attacks against Ordonians have been few and small, clearly the work of a single group. Everyone else has accepted defeat and moved on."

"Accepted defeat! Nothing is lost yet!" Helen cried, eliciting a confused look in response.

"Apparently information has been as scarce to you as soap. Go and get your friends. They need to hear what I have to tell you, and I'm not interested in repeating myself," Reuben told her, then closed the door.

"What are you talking about?" Helen screamed, then kicked the door upon not receiving a reply. She obviously wasn't going to get anything else out of him, so she stormed off back to the truck and left to retrieve the others.

Dodge Family Residence
4:21 P.M.

"This can't be right. We would never surrender," Helen declared.

"Well, we did. The union is gone, and it's time for us to get on with our lives. Speaking of, I have work to do," Reuben responded, then got up and left the room to leave the team standing or sitting in stunned silence.

"Guess there's no reason to fight now," Exodus observed.

"There's plenty of reason to fight. The Ordonians are no less tyrants now than they were before," Helen countered.

"The war is over, and we lost. There's nothing we can do now."

"We can do a lot. We don't need some cowardly government behind us to fight for what we believe!"

"I believe in staying alive."

"So you're willing to be a slave for the rest of your life for the sake of being able to keep breathing!" Helen challenged, rising from her chair in the process.

"That's enough!" Breise shouted, then stared at the captain until she retook her seat.

"We can't do anything until we regather our strength and restock our supplies," Nafais suggested.

"Muddie's right. I say we table the discussion of whether or not to keep fighting until we've rested up. None of us are in the right frame of mind to be making big decisions," Breise agreed.

"So what *are* we going to do?" Helen questioned.

"Let's start with you showing us where we'll be sleeping and where we can get cleaned up. I don't know about the rest of you, but I'm ready to rid myself of a year's worth of dirt and sweat," the major responded, eliciting a few chuckles from the team, even a quick snort from Helen.

Chapter Nine
Destroy Black Tempest

Red Command
Tactical Center
Thursday, January 2nd, 2708
8:31 A.M.

His little brother had come a long way since last they met. When he'd deserted from the union fleet, Sam was a mere lieutenant who had never taken part in creating or implementing strategies, yet now Leon found himself reviewing a solid strategy crafted almost entirely by the younger Tyquese.

Their enemy was a powerful pirate captain, but the territory she controlled on this planet was small, at least when compared to targets the Vehlan soldiers were accustomed to assaulting.

"My forces are in position. Three companies at each of the north, west, and east borders. Are you sure they are in no danger from the other factions?" Leon relayed.

"Yes, I'm sure. There is a sizable no-man's land between the territories. Makes everybody a little more comfortable that way," Sam responded, his annoyance plain at having to explain this again.

"And your troops are capable of holding the southern border?"

"That's their job, regardless of any attack. And before you ask, the hornet riders won't let us down, either. They live for this sort of thing," Sam maintained, referencing the hover bikes used by all pirate factions as a quick attack vehicle.

"Let's do this," Leon incited, and Sam relayed the order to the field commanders.

The Vehlans began marching towards Tempest's perimeter, accompanied by tanks and miniature defense drones. The drone weapons were ineffective in an offense, but they would serve to exaggerate their numbers.

When the war got bad for their side, Leon had suggested hiding some equipment on various planets to be at the disposal of any units caught behind the lines. They'd only managed to recover these drones and a few tanks thus far, but it was enough for this attack.

"It's starting," Sam observed.

Black Border Outpost 2
8:44 A.M.

Border duty, again.

A pirate was meant to be mobile, raiding convoys and bar-hopping, not sitting around staring at an empty desert. If he'd wanted to do that, he could have joined the military back home. Who was ever going to attack them anyway?

However, Captain Tempest insisted an officer be stationed on the border to keep an eye on things, and Sergeant Natine was the lucky one chosen. So day after day, he went from one outpost to the next ensuring procedures, however limited, were followed and no threats were detected.

So much for seeking a life of adventure.

His duties concluded for now, he was standing on the roof of the base's command unit when he thought he saw a dust cloud out in the desert.

"Are we detecting anything on sensors?" he radioed down to the control room.

"Negative," the watch officer responded with a yawn.

Then he saw several flashes of light within the dust, and seconds later a growing whistling noise filled the air.

"Take cover!" he shouted to no one in particular, then dove to the rooftop.

He covered his head and pressed himself down as flat as he could while explosions rocked the outpost.

When the ground stopped shaking, he crawled to the edge to survey the damage. There wasn't a lot, but that was of little comfort. Both of their laser cannons were gone along with two of their rapid-fire laser gun emplacements.

The whistles of another volley caused him to roll back onto the roof and cover himself again. This time a round struck close enough to shower him with small debris, and he went scrambling to the door and inside before anything else could happen.

"Report!"

"We are under attack from all sides, except the south!"

"I thought you said there was nothing on sensors!"

"There wasn't! There still isn't! They must be jamming us!"

"Do we know who it is?"

"How can we know that without sensors?" the watch officer smarted off, then held up a hand for silence as he flattened the other against his ear to muffle the sound of more explosions.

"The captain just ordered the EMP Cannons to fire on enemy position."

"They're out of range."

"Recent upgrades have doubled their range."

"Whatever. I'll take it."

Eastern Flank
Vehlan Forces
9:03 A.M.

The tanks fired again, and Private Olian couldn't help but wonder what was taking so long. Since they didn't have any Missile Tanks, they'd retrofitted the Lion Tanks for long-range artillery firing, but they still should have been able to level a pirate outpost in one or two volleys. This was the fourth one, yet they still hadn't been given the order to move in.

Then he saw two balls of lightning fly by overhead and strike the tanks, but they were unaffected and fired again as if to show that to the enemy.

"I know you were hoping to stand around doing nothing all day, but there's work to be done here! Charge!" Olian's lieutenant joked.

The soldiers cheered, then ran forward as fast as they could, taking the defense drones with them but leaving the tanks where they were. They were careful to run as individuals and not in formation as a regular military force should. Best to avoid letting anyone know who they really were for the time being.

Black Border Outpost 2
9:09 A.M.

"The EMPs didn't work!"

"Thanks for letting me know. I'd never have figured it out on my own," Natine retorted.

"Look!" another pirate shouted, and Natine followed his pointing finger to see a video screen showing dozens of soldiers running towards them. The defenders started shooting with whatever they had left, but their shots were swallowed up by the superior fire coming back at them.

"What's happening at the other borders?"

"Same thing as here! There's thousands of 'em!"

The sergeant let out a string of curses, then grabbed his rifle and ran for the door.

"Everyone fall back to the main base!" he ordered via comlink as he ran.

Once outside, he rushed to his personal Hornet hover bike and jumped aboard, barely realizing all the bikes should have been destroyed in the artillery attack.

He sped away towards the main base at the center of their territory, never bothering to see if the others made it out. Minutes later he spotted dozens of bikes speeding towards him from the left, but figured they were his own people and didn't pay much attention.

Then their passengers started shooting at him, causing him and those with him to turn aside in surprise. The attackers exploited this to get in between them and the main base.

"Head north!" Natine shouted, then led the way.

If they could move fast enough, they would meet up with the northern defenders and push through to the base before the attackers could cut them off again. With a little luck, the western defenders would do the same thing, then they would be able to use their numbers to push through even if they did get cut off.

Luck was not theirs to have.

They met up with several of the pirates who had been defending the northern border only to find them also being chased.

Natine braked hard, and frantically looked around, desperate to find an escape, but there wasn't one to be found.

The pursuers on bikes surrounded them, and the enemy infantry could be seen forming up in the distance.

Now that they were closer, Natine could see the red armbands on the bike riders, marking them as Red Sam's pirates. Their sergeant smiled from the backseat of his bike, and jerked his rifle towards the ground, indicating for them to throw down their weapons.

Disgusted, but seeing no choice, Natine obeyed and the others followed his lead.

Red Command
Tactical Center
9:24 A.M.

The last of the border defenders surrendered, and Sam's pirates began hauling them back to their territory while Leon's soldiers established a siege perimeter around Tempest's main base.

When the Vehlans opened fire on their targets, Sam had sent the majority of his own forces against the southern border, capturing it quickly. Most of them had then climbed aboard their Hornet bikes and raced into black territory, managing to make it even as far as the northern sections to cut off the retreating border guards after Leon's people routed them.

That took nearly half of Black Tempest's pirates out of the picture with almost no casualties on their side.

"Good work," Leon commented.

"We're not done yet. There's still the main base and Tempest herself to capture," Sam responded gruffly, carefully hiding his pride at receiving a compliment from his difficult to please older brother.

"Then let's get out there and get it done."

Joint Command Position
Southern Flank
9:47 A.M.

"All primary and secondary artillery targets confirmed destroyed, sir," Captain Mathison reported as the Tyquese brothers approached.

"Good work, Captain," Leon commended, then stepped to the front of the formation to get a better look at the base.

He lowered his helmet visor over his eyes, activated its zoom function, and studied the enemy fortifications. Their design was the same as those protecting Sam's base, except these towers were now smoking pillars. The walls were still intact, but wouldn't pose a challenge.

Once he was satisfied all was going according to plan, he raised the visor and turned to Mathison.

"Captain Tyquese and I are going to personally lead the final push into the enemy base. Target breach points in the walls and await my signal," he ordered, then took up position at the head of the formation with Sam on his left. They had formed this company out of two platoons, one Vehlan and one pirate.

They began marching towards the base, and their soldiers automatically followed them. Leon decided now was as good a time as any to confide in his brother.

"I want you to know that I have always believed in you, Sam. I know I pressured you a lot when we were younger, but it was only because I knew you were capable of so much more than you ever attempted on your own. I don't agree with many of your decisions, but I never gave up on you, not even when you deserted and became a pirate. You will always be my brother."

The steady sound of marching filled the air, but Sam didn't say anything for a long time, causing Leon to wonder if he should say more.

"I appreciate you telling me that, and I feel the same towards you. I gave up on the union and thought you should too, but I've always respected you. There was even a part of me that was jealous you were able to remain loyal through it all."

"The union turned its back on its ideals, and you saw that before I did. I reached a point where I wasn't fighting for the nation anymore, but remained where I was because I still saw it as the best place to fight for my own beliefs. That is what keeps me going."

"I still believe the union should remain dead, and that Vehla itself has no place in our efforts, but I do believe in the same things you do. I just gave up hope on them ever being reality."

"We will make it a reality," Leon decreed as he held up his right fist to signal a halt.

He checked the tactical screen on his palco, a microcomputer embedded in his left hand which displayed a holographic screen when activated, saw that all units were in position, and gave the order for Mathison to open fire.

The laser rounds blasted above their heads and struck the wall, sending up clouds of fire, smoke, and debris, enough to obscure their view of the base. They didn't wait for it to clear.

"Breach now!" they ordered simultaneously via comlink, then took off running.

They charged through the walls shooting, training and experience keeping them from choking in the smoke and dust. A few brave souls returned fire, but quickly fell to their onslaught and the rest either ran or surrendered.

This continued until they reached the command center, at which point the brothers halted the attack long enough to establish a perimeter and bring the tanks into range.

"What defenses should we be expecting?" Leon asked.

"Nothing fancy. Just more pirates," Sam replied.

"No shields or automated guns?"

"Pirate captains consider such things to be a waste of money because they are almost never needed. There's a sensor grid, but I have a feeling she already knows we're here."

"I didn't expect it to be this easy," Leon brooded, after which he received a signal that the tanks were in position.

"No faction is capable of mounting a defense against our combined numbers, and this isn't exactly typical warfare for us. Once I take control of Tempest's forces, the other factions won't be able to oppose us even if they banded together," Sam reassured him.

At an order from Leon, the tanks fired a single volley on the command center, punching several holes in its walls while leaving structural integrity intact.

The attackers swarmed inside where they encountered some real resistance, but they swept aside all in their path and within minutes the brothers found themselves in the command center.

They secured the room, but found no sign of their adversary.

"Did she escape somehow?" Leon questioned.

"That's not possible, assuming your people did their job right," Sam responded from his position in the center of the room. He slowly spun in place, looking around for something he might have missed.

"Underground tunnels?"

"There aren't any."

"How can you be sure?"

"Because I stole a scout ship from the union and used it to scan all the bases on this planet. They have underground storage, but no escape tunnels," Sam explained, and Leon ceased his search of the room to stare at him.

"You stole a ship from the union?"

"Don't act so surprised. Once I defected and became a pirate, union property became fair game same as everyone else's. Before you ask, the crew is fine."

The colonel considered demanding the identities of all former union personnel in his brother's employ so he could take command of them, but then thought better of it. Sam would just say they were pirates now with no obligation to Leon or any other union officer, and he would be right.

"Then where did Black Tempest go? What would you do in this situation?" he asked instead.

"I wouldn't have let it get this far in the first place, and Tempest and I don't think at all alike. We'll have to think like her, not me," Sam responded, then groaned in sudden realization.

"What?"

"I just realized that if I ever did get into a situation such as this, I would have to use the tactics I'm most familiar with. Follow me," he explained, then hurriedly left the room.

Their forces had secured nearly the entire command center, so they had no trouble reaching their destination one floor above. Upon exiting the stairwell, they saw a set of double doors to their left, which Sam casually opened and strolled through. Leon followed and found that they were in the sitting room of a bedroom suite.

"Ah, Red Sam. So nice of you to stop by. Come and join me in here," a woman's voice called from the other room. Sam went to follow the voice, but Leon stopped him with a hand on his shoulder.

"Are you sure that's wise?" he asked in a low tone.

"It isn't her intent to kill us. She knows it wouldn't do any good," Sam responded, then shrugged off the hand and went through the door on the right side of the room, Leon right on his heels.

They entered to discover a brown-haired woman standing with her back to them. She tossed a pair of armored pants on the floor, then turned to face them, wearing only a one-piece set of underarmor.

"If you wanted to see me this badly, all you had to do was say so, although I must admit, I do find this display of raw power stimulating," she greeted them.

"Save it, Tempest. I'm not as stupid as the man you killed to steal everything he had," Sam snapped.

"And you brought a friend with you, too. No, not just a friend. I can see the family resemblance. Older brother, perhaps?" Tempest cooed, looking towards Leon. She smiled slyly, and began walking towards him.

"I can see it now. The air of authority, confidence, and experience. I knew you were incapable of defeating me without help from one such as this."

She stopped a few inches in front of him and looked up into his eyes. He met her gaze, but kept alert for any attacks.

"You don't have to keep working with him just because he's your brother. Why don't you see what I have to offer?" she suggested, then reached up to stroke his face, but he stopped her by grabbing her wrist.

"I am a colonel in the Vehlan military. I have no interest in anything you have to offer."

"The Vehlan Union no longer exists. There must be a reason you chose to ally yourself with pirates," Tempest wondered aloud. Leon spotted a note of desperation in her eyes, but it quickly disappeared as realization dawned on her.

"Of course! You're building a resistance movement against the Ordeon Empire. I promise you my techniques are far better for hurting them than any Red."

"Even if you didn't end up betraying me, such techniques have only the power to destroy. I cannot rebuild on a corrupt foundation, so like my brother said, save it!" Leon insisted, then released her arm with a shove that sent her stumbling backward.

"You'll fail! You don't have what it takes! You already lost once, and will again!" she shouted, her calmness melting into terror.

"Wrong. We won. You lost," Sam refuted, then spoke over his shoulder to his pirates on the other side of the door, "Bind her, gag her, and take her back to base."

She swore at them and backed away from them as if to run or fight, but then she tripped over the armor and fell backward onto the floor. Several pirates swarmed her and yanked her arms behind her back and tied them while another grabbed a shirt from the closet and shoved it in her mouth.

They hauled her up, then practically dragged her out of the room, kicking and screaming through the gag. Leon ordered five of his own soldiers to go with them and make sure they didn't mistreat her.

"This base is yours now. Do whatever you need to, then meet me back at my base in one hour," Sam told Leon once she was gone, then he left without waiting for a response.

Red Command Center
10:57 A.M.

The two pirate captains stared at each other as they waited for Leon to arrive so the broadcast could begin. Red Sam stood over Black Tempest where she had been forced to kneel on the floor, still bound and gagged.

Where others would be gloating in their moment of triumph, Sam felt more or less neutral. He didn't feel any hatred towards his rival, and defeating her registered as little more than removing an obstacle to his plans.

Her feelings were quite the opposite, made clear by the burning in her dark green eyes as she glared into his.

The colonel finally entered, exactly on time, and surveyed the scene with a disapproving frown.

"No matter what happens here, go with it. We are pirates, not soldiers, and must do things a certain way," Sam told him before he could say anything.

His brother looked at him, hesitated a moment, but then responded with a short nod and took up position by the wall.

11:00 A.M.

The pirates began the broadcast, and Leon watched as Sam stood behind Tempest and bragged about defeating her.

There was no denying what was about to happen. His ethics told him he should stop this, but in his heart he knew it was necessary. He was playing under a different set of rules now, and had to abide by them to have any chance of achieving his goals.

Still, he couldn't help but wonder if he was making the same mistake as the union during the war. Was he turning his back on his principles, and justifying it by saying that victory was more important?

As Sam neared the end of his speech, Leon realized there was only one thing he could do and left the room.

11:09 A.M.

His brother left before he could finish, but Sam didn't care. Piracy was a dirty business, and he was going to have to get over it.

"Now that I have control of the black faction and all its resources, none of you can stand against me. Submit to my authority within twenty-four hours, or the same will happen to you," he concluded, then pulled out his pistol and shot Tempest in the back of the head.

"Twenty-four hours," he repeated, then holstered his pistol and exited the room.

Red Command Center
Captain's Suite
4:53 P.M.

Sam walked onto his balcony and found his brother on a lounge chair watching the sunset.

"Have they all signed on?" Leon asked after Sam walked up to stand on his right.

"All but two, Green Simon and Brown Nick. I have no doubt that Simon will submit, even if it's at the last minute. Nick is another story, however."

"Why is that?"

"Greens are information dealers, so I'm sure Simon only wants to learn as much as he can about how I defeated Tempest before I assume control of his intelligence gathering assets. The brown faction is known for having the best defenses around their facilities, so Nick may think he has a chance to resist."

"Does he?"

"No. He probably knows that already, and is simply trying to save face. If he doesn't, we'll just have to destroy him."

The elder brother sighed, then stood to face his brother in the deepening shadows.

"I understand it was necessary to execute Black Tempest. She was too dangerous alive, and you needed to prove your resolve to the other captains, but it must never happen again. Any future prisoners, regardless of who or what they are, will be treated properly."

"That philosophy can't work here! How many times do I have to tell you this? These are pirates, and if I am going to lead them, I must act like one of them!" Sam argued.

"Yes, they are pirates, but most of them came from either the Vehlan or Ordonian militaries. Like you, they deserted because they didn't want to fight in the war for one reason or another. They can, and should, act with more discipline."

"Discipline. Protocol. Ethics. We left all of that behind when we jumped ship."

"That's not true. I've seen you with your pirates. You still expect all those things out of them. Not in the same way as the union did, but you still expect them to follow a code of conduct, and they do it."

"That's different."

"How?" Leon challenged. Sam started to reply, but stopped himself. Possible answers rushed through his mind, but all of them sounded hollow, even to him.

Leon continued, "Most here only wanted to escape the war, and were labeled criminals as a result. A life of crime became your only means to survive, but I am here to offer you hope for the future."

Still unable to think of a response, Sam sighed, walked to the balcony rail and leaned on it to stare out across the stony desert, now fully shrouded in night. Leon joined him there.

"I ignored one of my core beliefs today to achieve an objective, which is something I swore I would never do. You deserted the union because it turned its back on its principles, all of which you personally value, yet now you've done the same thing. How long before we come to the same end?"

"Never."

"That's right, because from this moment forward we hold true to what we believe, no matter how hard it gets. We will rebuild properly, and on a secure foundation."

"Agreed," Sam responded. Strangely, he felt as if a weight had lifted from him and he could now breathe easier. As if he had been pretending to be someone he was not, and was now rediscovering himself.

A laser suddenly shot over their heads, causing Leon to dive to the floor.

"What's that? Are we under attack?" he exclaimed, but the only response he received was hysterical laughter. Sam had to brace himself against the rail to keep from collapsing from his mirth.

"Why are you laughing?" Leon questioned as he stood up again, but it was some time before Sam could catch his breath to respond.

"Oh, I really wish I had a video of that."

"I fail to see what is so funny."

"My bug zapper scared you," Sam explained and pointed to a device above the door.

"You use a mini defense drone as a bug zapper?"

"There are some pretty big bugs on this planet, and they aren't pleasant. I would rather kiss the emperor's feet than let any of them near me," Sam told him as he headed into the rooms.

"Must be some pretty nasty bugs," Leon commented as he sat down.

Sam grabbed a pair of wine glasses and a bottle of fine wine, then returned to the balcony where he filled the glasses before taking a seat.

The two of them then proceeded to discuss the details of their new organization. They agreed to call it the Pirate League and to create a new flag for it, one which would have the ancient Jolly Roger symbol with blue stars for eyes and rifles in place of swords or bones.

On the matter of command, they decided to maintain separate jurisdiction over their own groups. Sam was in charge of the pirates and Leon the soldiers, with neither one having the authority to give orders to the other.

The pirate captains would be allowed to keep their commands and holdings, with the only thing changing for them the requirement to report to Sam as the final authority. Thirty percent of anything the factions stole was to go to Leon and Sam, but they could earn a reduced tribute for loyalty and skill.

It was well into the night before they finished, but each left feeling they had established a strong baseline for themselves and those they led.

Chapter Ten
Those Who Came Before

Altaius
Resistance Base
Saturday, January 11th, 2708
5:00 P.M.

"As the sun sets on this day, we gather to remember the sacrifice of those who came before. Countless men and women have died in the cause of hope. Hope for a future free of oppression and tyranny, and maybe even free of war," Colonel Tyquese addressed his troops.

All two-thousand of them had gathered in the field outside their new base for this ceremony, dressed in freshly polished armor proudly bearing their union markings. He stood in front of them on a makeshift stage with an honor guard carrying union flags standing at attention behind him.

They were taking a risk displaying their true colors like this, but the colonel knew they needed to take some time to honor the fallen. This was the safest they had been since escaping Vehla, and there was no telling when they would get another chance. Besides, Sam had promised to keep all prying eyes away.

"We all know people who gave the ultimate sacrifice. Let us take a moment of silence to remember our brothers and sisters in arms," he continued.

The setting sun to his left cast an orange glow over the gathering, but there was just enough light left for him to peer into the faces of his soldiers as they stood in reflection. There were no tears, but there was a profound sadness as everyone recalled friends and family members who had fallen in battle.

"I refuse to believe these brave souls died for nothing. Our nation has fallen, but its ideals live on in us. We must hold onto those ideals and never lose hope, or those sacrifices will be rendered meaningless. Tonight, we remember those who fought and died before us. Soon, we will honor them by continuing to fight for what we believe."

He took one last, long look at those gathered before him, then pivoted on one heel to face the flags, where he then came to attention and brought his right hand to forehead in salute. A loud rustling told him the crowd was also saluting, then the national anthem played on a mobile device.

When the anthem finished, Leon slowly dropped his hand forward, then spun around and brought it up again to salute his soldiers.

Two sets of honor guards, one on either side of the crowd, fired three times into the air, and Leon thrust his hand forward in conclusion.

"I am granting you a reprieve from your duties for tomorrow. Rest and enjoy yourselves as much as you can. Monday, we return to the task before us."

Chapter Eleven
Lost Histories

Friday, January 17th, 2708
6:32 P.M.

In their quarters at the center of their respective operations, Colonel Tyquese and Primary Canza each sat down to read the book given to them by their superiors. All Tyquese had was a simple notebook written by General Reno, but Canza had a traditionally published volume titled, "Lost Histories of Humanity".

The business of survival and strategy had kept them too busy to stop and read a book, but now it was time to find out what was so important.

Lost Histories of Humanity
Introduction

Our history starts seventy years prior to this writing. At least, that's where it starts in the public record. We are told that everything before that was lost during the Time of Chaos while the nations were being formed and before they could act to preserve our past.

This is a lie.

There is no denying the Time of Chaos itself, a period of decades where the human race faced its end, but then overcame it. However, it was not the catastrophes we endured that destroyed our history, but rather it was our own governments who sought to cover up our sins. Officially, no one knows the nature of the cataclysm behind the Time of Chaos. This is another lie.

When we first discovered space travel and spread out amongst the stars, we were not the only form of sapient life. There were alien civilizations, and we co-existed with them for a time.

Then one day, many of them attacked us. I do not know the reason for the attack, only that it happened and that defeat was inevitable. The nations were created to fight this threat from multiple angles, and we eventually prevailed, but it did not end there.

The desire for survival and justice grew into a lust for power and revenge, and most of the new governments decreed that all aliens be exterminated. Not only the ones who had attacked us, but all forms of non-human sapient life. They claimed it was the only way to ensure humanity's safety, and the people went along with it. So the killing began, and continued until there was no longer any trace of alien civilization.

It is also taught that knowledge of the origin point of the human race was lost with everything else, but this is also untrue.

We originated on Earth, a planet now believed to be a myth, but it did exist once. It was lost shortly after the genocides began. I could not find out how or why, but it's possible that it is still out there, inhabited by our kin.

I have spent many years and endured many trials in my search for the truth, and now I present my findings to you. No government wants this information to get out. It is the one thing they all agree on, but I must try.

Here is all that remains of our history before our current age. No matter how bad it may be, or how difficult it is to accept, we must remember what came before.

-Arcon Sleise

7:03 P.M.

The news of what their ancestors had done struck both men like a bolt of lightning.

Human civilization existed on hundreds of planets orbiting dozens of stars, but only because they were the inheritors of a legacy of genocide.

Could they ever truly be free drowning in oceans of blood?

Was there such a thing as a glorious future while this existed in the past?

Chapter Twelve
A New Campaign

OES Dragon's Breath
Monday, January 20th, 2708
7:51 A.M.

His inspection rounds complete, Primary Canza entered the bridge and headed straight to the captain's chair.

"Tactical display," he ordered as he sat down. The ship's captain came up to stand beside him in the position of ship's first officer, his role as long as the primary was aboard.

The main screen at the front of the bridge lit up to display their target, the first system in their campaign to seize the Merchant's Interest. Its central planet was called Culture Blend, and it was best described as a planetary theme park.

Since it bordered the union, the merchant government figured it was a place where all the nations could be represented, starting with those that comprised the union but eventually showcasing others as well. Each nation was invited to build a town on the planet which exemplified their culture, then people could come and visit any nation they wanted all in one place.

Participating nations received a share of anything tourists spent in their towns, but the Ordeon Empire was one of the few to choose not to build a town. Anyone who wanted to visit them was welcome to come to the real thing, not some fake designed to satisfy someone else's greed.Except soon, this place would be a part of the real thing.

"Emperor's speech coming through now, sir," Communications reported from his right. He nodded in response, and the tactical display disappeared to be replaced by the broadcast.

"All nations, take heed. This transmission comes to you directly from the royal palace on Ordeos Prime. The esteemed Emperor Johan Lentaise has a critical announcement to make," a herald introduced, then stepped aside to reveal the emperor who was decked out in his best regalia and standing behind a podium emblazoned with the imperial seal depicting the first emperor and the civilization he created.

"Citizens of humanity, I bring you disturbing news this day. We believed the threat to our future finally ended with the destruction of the Vehlan Union one month ago, but we were wrong.

"We have learned that many Vehlan military personnel escaped into the Merchant's Interest, taking with them a large amount of equipment and ships. They have rejected our lawful rule, and our generous offer of amnesty, and seek to strike out at us and threaten the peace and stability we have established.

"The interest chose to shelter these criminals, and as such share in their guilt. We did not end the Hundred Years War to face living under the constant threat of terrorism, and will not sit quietly by while our enemies seek to harm us.

"In the interest of protecting my people and our dreams for the future, I have decided to annex the Merchant's Interest. Its leaders will be arrested and replaced with those dedicated to peace and the rule of law, and all Vehlan criminals will be brought to justice. This decision was not made lightly as I do not want to send more of my citizens to die, but I remember that their sacrifice will bring us the future of peace and prosperity which we all desire," Lentaise proclaimed.

On cue, Canza ordered his fleet to move to the target coordinates. If all went as planned, they would arrive at the conclusion of the emperor's speech.

"Despite previous rejections of our kindness, I still wish to extend an offer of mercy to all former Vehlan military personnel and those harboring them. Turn yourselves in along with all stolen military equipment, and you will receive a reduced sentence. Cooperate with us by supplying information, and you may receive a full pardon.

"Anyone else that has committed no crime but may have information to aid us in our mission, you will be greatly rewarded for bringing that information to us.

"I sincerely hope everyone will make the correct choices during these troubled times. We do not wish to kill and destroy, nor do we wish to die, but we are willing to do what it takes to secure the future. The consequences will be on your own heads," the emperor finished just as Canza's fleet dropped out of hyperspace.

They immediately fired a volley at the defensive satellites orbiting the planet, destroying them before they could react.

"Surround the planet."

"Vehlan ships moving in on intercept course, sir. One destroyer and five corvettes."

"Weapons and shields?"

"Armed, sir."

"A suicide run? Why?" the captain questioned.

"Open a general channel," Canza ordered. "This is the Ordonian Dreadnaught Dragon's Breath to approaching Vehlan ships. You are outnumbered and outgunned. Surrender, or be destroyed."

He glanced at Communications, but the officer only shook his head to indicate they weren't receiving a response.

"Don't be stupid. You will be treated fairly if you surrender. You heard the emperor's speech, so you know this offer comes directly from him. There is no need for you to die."

"Our nation may be gone, but that doesn't mean you've changed. You make fancy speeches about peace, prosperity, and mercy for anyone who bows down before you, but we know better. Our lives are forfeit one way or the other. We'd rather die fighting for freedom than be executed in some back room."

"Your death here will accomplish nothing. It will be meaningless," Canza argued, but the only response was a laser barrage.

"Very well, then," he concluded, then signaled to cut the channel.

"All ships: return fire. Fire at will," the captain ordered. Canza would normally command directly and employ more strategy, but the enemy was so weak there really was no point.

He watched the main screen as his ships opened fire, nearly obscuring the enemy under the barrage of white plasma bolts. They stopped less than a minute later, revealing clouds of dust and debris. All that was left of the enemy.

"Establish orbit. Launch ground invasion."

Again, he chose not to lead the assault personally. The ground defenses weren't enough to warrant the effort on his part.

The planet was under their control an hour later and his forces were setting up their new forward base. Per protocol, they didn't have all the construction materials with them, preferring to dedicate that space to combat equipment, so he gave the order for the supply ships to deploy from behind the line.

His work here done, Canza left the captain to manage the details and went to the tactical room behind the bridge to double check their campaign plan.

They would normally work slowly, securing every occupied planet, moon, and asteroid in a system before moving on to the next one, but this time he and the emperor had settled on a blitz approach. The primary would attack the central planet in each system, secure, then move on to do the same in the next system.

Once they had the merchant homeworld under their control, the rest would fall in line.

Altaius
Resistance Spaceport
9:33 A.M.

After capturing this base from Black Tempest, the Vehlans had refortified it into a proper military installation by rebuilding the walls and replacing the towers with gun emplacements. This activity had garnered the attention of the pirates and they'd caught members from each faction snooping around, but so far they seemed to believe the story that they were nothing more than a mercenary outfit hired by Red Sam.

Once he was satisfied their position was safe, Leon had turned their attention towards enacting their resistance movement against the Ordonians. The emperor's speech had accelerated their efforts because he wouldn't have revealed his intentions unless he was already prepared to strike, but they should still have enough time to get ready.

"Colonel, call for you from Red Sam," Captain Mathison reported via comlink from the command center.

"Patch it to my location," Leon responded, then helped a soldier set down a heavy load before heading to the terminal in the hangar.

"What is it?" he asked.

"The empire has launched and already won its first attack against the Merchant's Interest. It looks like it was coordinated to begin exactly when the emperor's speech ended."

"How long since they secured the planet? Not just orbit, but the ground as well?"

"A few minutes."

Leon slapped the terminal, causing those around him to glance at him before quickly returning to their work.

The empire was still changing its tactics, and once again he was caught unprepared.

He knew that upon capturing a planet, the Ordonians always sent out a supply convoy from their nearest holding with materials for building a new base. There was only one place which they could launch this convoy from, and he wanted to seize it.

It would take the convoy about a day to reach the ambush point, but their own travel time wasn't much faster. If they were going to make it, they would have to leave within the hour.

"We are not going to miss this opportunity! I want our assault force in space within forty-five minutes!" he declared.

He expected his brother to insist this wasn't possible, but he only smiled and cut the connection.

The colonel then turned back towards the hangar and shouted at them to have their craft ready in forty minutes. Everyone kicked it into high-gear knowing he would never raise his voice like that unless it was really serious.

Next, he activated his earpiece and ordered Captain Mathison to have the soldiers for the mission geared up and on their transports within thirty minutes.

He was not going to let the Imps get the better of him again.

Ordeos Prime
Royal Palace
12:08 P.M.

Upon entering the pool area of the palace with her two children, Prailia spotted her husband on the other side of the pool receiving a massage.

"Go ahead. You can join me when the food is ready," she told the kids, then smiled when they shouted with joy and jumped into the water. They were princes with all the expectations and responsibility that came with the role, but they were still young and full of life. As they grew older, they would receive ever increasing responsibility, but for now they still had some freedom to enjoy themselves.

She looked back towards the emperor to see him watching her through slitted eyes.

"I heard the primary seized Culture Blend almost without a fight," she stated upon walking up to him.

"They pose no challenge."

"True," she responded, then fell silent. Servants set out lunch on the other side of the room while the boys laughed and played in the pool.

"What do you want?" Johan finally asked.

"I think it's time for me to go on a goodwill tour of the provinces, and I want the children to join me."

"Why?"

"While you continue working to destroy our enemies and expand the empire, I need to see to the needs of our people. Their biggest need during our operations in foreign territories is to know we have not forgotten them. Where the princes are concerned, it will be good for them to see more of the empire they will one day rule."

"They have studies."

"Their tutors will be with us."

"Fine. Go." Johan granted.

"Lunch is ready, Majesty," a servant reported.

"Will you join us?" Prailia asked her husband.

"I'm busy."

She shrugged, then called to the princes and joined them at the table where they discussed the adventure that awaited them.

Chapter Thirteen
From Law to Outlaw

Lead Pirate Boarding Vessel
Tuesday, January 21st, 2708
9:46 A.M.

"Any ships in the area?" Leon asked once they exited hyperspace.

"Target is three minutes out, but there is nothing else, sir," the pilot reported. Not a lot of time to get ready, but it would be enough.

"You know the plan. Get in position," Sam ordered from beside his brother.

The fifteen Stinger Assault Fighters took up position around where the convoy would exit hyperspace, and the boarding vessels moved a minute's distance away from the action. Most of the fighters were controlled by pirates, but Leon had insisted five of them be his own people.

Vehlan soldiers aboard the transports donned full face masks and each had removed identifying symbols from his/her armor. The Ordonians would likely still peg them as Vehlans, but at least this way they wouldn't be able to identify them as any specific 'criminal'.

Ship sensors were unable to read anything in normal space while the ship was in hyperspace, preventing the approaching convoy from detecting them until it was too late.

They had chosen this location because a local phenomenon known as the Hyperspace Vortex forced ships to travel through normal space for a while or be torn apart. To stay in hyperspace and go around added half a day of travel time, but dropping out and proceeding through the same section in normal space only added four hours.

As an important route between the union and interest, the former had always maintained heavy patrols in the area to keep away anyone who would take advantage of time-conscious travelers, but Leon was confident that the empire did not yet see a need for this.

It was possible to fight in hyperspace, but people rarely did. Intense radiation required ships to divert nearly all their power to the shields, and the engines used most of what was left over leaving practically nothing for the weapons. Aggressors normally found a way to draw out their targets, and anyone who did happen to come under attack while inside, usually dropped to normal space to have the best chance at defending themselves.

The oddest thing about the phenomenon was that no one knew what caused it. Some scientists even believed it to have an artificial origin, but none dared to guess at who could have created it or why.

"In position," the lead fighter pilot reported. Leon let Sam take charge at this point as he was the one with experience in such matters.

The timing was perfect, for as soon as the pilot's report came through the convoy appeared in front of them.

"Attack!"

All of the Stingers fired missiles, but the convoy's escort of ten Blade Light Fighters reacted quickly and moved to destroy them. Five missiles made it through the defense with four of them destroying enemy fighters while the fifth disabled a transport's engines.

The remaining blades engaged the pirates while the transports turned to escape, but it was too late. Eleven of the stingers dealt with the escort while the remaining four swooped in behind the transports and disabled them.

When it was over, three more of the blades were destroyed, the rest were disabled, and the pirates had taken only minor damage. One of the pirate boarding craft worked on getting the pilots out of the disabled fighters while the rest descended on the supply ships.

Mere minutes after arriving in the system, Leon found himself on an Ordonian transport staring into a rifle barrel. He made no move to disarm the guard or draw his pistol, but simply stared at him until he finally realized there was nothing he could do and lowered his weapon.

"Get all this stuff loaded up," he ordered the soldiers and pirates behind him. The cargo hold was filled with wall, ceiling, and floor panels for a prefabricated building, exactly what he'd hoped to find.

This particular building was likely intended to be an armory as along with the panels they also found two large storage chests, one filled with weapons and the other with armor. Icing on the cake.

"Well now, what do we have here?" a voice pondered from the cockpit. The colonel decided to investigate.

"Let go of me!" he heard a female voice exclaim as he entered. The first thing he saw was a female Ordonian pilot struggling with one pirate while another watched, laughing.

"What? Are you too stuck up to have some fun with a pirate, Imp?" the bystander jeered as his buddy threw the woman to the floor.

Before he could do anything else, Leon grabbed the aggressor by the shoulder, turned him around, and punched him in his unprotected face, knocking him to the floor with the force of the blow.

"What are you doing?" the bystander shouted and raised his rifle to point at Leon. His buddy remained on the floor rubbing his jaw, too stunned to do anything.

A Vehlan soldier came in, saw a pirate threatening his colonel, smacked the rifle out of his hands, then pushed him against a wall and held a pistol to his chin.

"Stay here," Leon told the woman, then he pulled the first pirate off the floor and dragged him back into the cargo area while his soldier followed with the other one.

"What's going on here?" Sam demanded to know when he saw two of his men being manhandled by Vehlans.

"I caught this one attempting to rape the pilot while his buddy here watched!" Leon sneered, and shoved his prisoner towards Sam.

"Is this true?" Sam growled.

"Yeah, what of it?"

The captain studied the faces of both men, then quietly accused them of having formerly worked for Black Tempest, and the bystander confirmed it.

"Then I suppose I have to teach you another lesson."

He grabbed the would-be rapist and pulled him towards the back of the ship while Leon followed with his soldier and the other pirate.

Everyone else ignored them and continued unloading the ship.

When they reached the rear of the cargo hold, Sam shoved the pirate into the wall next to an airlock.

"Tempest allowed you to do whatever you wanted, but that's not going to be the case with me. I absolutely do not tolerate rape and despise anyone who would consider such an act," he explained, then hit the button to open the airlock's inner door.

The pirate began to struggle and shout for help, but no one came to his aid and Leon helped his brother push him into the airlock with a shove hard enough to throw him up against the outer door.

He tried to run back through, but Sam closed the inner door before he could and opened the outer door. There was a sucking sound, then the airlock was empty.

"Make sure the rest of your people learn what happened here, and that they know the same will happen to them if they misbehave," Sam told the bystander who was watching the scene wide-eyed. He nodded his understanding, and Sam ordered he be let go.

The rest of the mission continued in silence. They loaded everything onto their boarding craft, moved the transport crews and surviving fighter pilots to one of the craft, then attached towing cables to the disabled blades and two of the supply ships.

They headed back home, the pirates richer and the Vehlans equipped to renew the fight.

Culture Blend
11:08 A.M.

Earlier in the day, Primary Canza had shuttled down to the planet's surface to inspect their operations, and was currently observing the construction of their new base. The buildings were pre-fabricated in a factory back in the empire, but the foundations still needed to be built on site.

All was proceeding on schedule and should be ready by the time their supplies arrived, after which everything would be finished within hours.

"Primary Canza?"

"Yes, Lieutenant," he responded after turning around.

"We received word that our supply convoy was hit by pirates while crossing the hyperspace vortex, sir."

"How much damage did we receive?"

"The entire escort was disabled or destroyed, sir. They took all the cargo, two of the transports, and three Blades."

"How many pirates were destroyed?"

"None, sir."

Silence fell as the primary processed the news. It was little surprise the convoy had come under pirate attack, but for those criminals to succeed so completely without suffering heavy losses was another matter.

"Get me all the information we have on the pirates, and I want the survivors brought to my fleet for debriefing," he ordered. The lieutenant saluted and ran off to relay the message.

Canza then sent a separate message to Secondary Farra through his ship in orbit telling him to send another convoy and to have all ships go around the vortex until further notice. After one last check with the garrison commander, he returned to his dreadnaught and ordered the fleet to move out to the next target.

They would finish with the merchants soon enough, then the pirates would face Ordonian justice.

Chapter Fourteen
Contingency

Altaius
Red Command Center
Wednesday, January 22nd, 2708
12:12 P.M.

"What he did was wrong, but was it really necessary to space that man?" Leon asked once he and Sam were alone in the latter's office.

"Yes, it was. Pirates do not obey unless one is willing to enact the harshest of punishments."

"Brutality usually leads to mutiny."

"That's true in the military where respect is enough to earn obedience, but not among pirates where a mixture of respect and fear is required to maintain order. While we're on the subject of discipline, though, there's something I need to discuss with you."

"What's that?"

"We have to allow the other captains to choose their own targets and attack them as they see fit. If we don't let them carry on as they did before, with few exceptions such as yesterday, they will turn on us and kill us."

"The idea here is to hurt the empire while helping its victims. How are we to do that if we let the pirates attack whoever they want?"

"For one thing, the empire is the prime target right now, like you said when we first agreed to this. As for the other nations, they won't be any worse off than they were before."

The colonel turned away from his brother and leaned on a chair to consider what he was saying. He couldn't deny that his brother had a point, but it still felt like it would unravel all his plans. There was the execution of Black Tempest, then of the rapist, and now Sam was saying he needed to let the pirates run amuck? When were they going to stop sliding backward and start moving forward?

However, nothing would be accomplished if the pirates stabbed them in the back.

"Alright, I agree. They can raid targets from anyone the empire is not currently attacking. That means the Merchant's Interest is to be left alone."

"They aren't going to like that. The interest has always been one of our richest sources."

"Tough.""Don't forget that I maintain direct command of the pirates. I could ignore you and tell them whatever I want."

"You shouldn't forget that you only have that command because of me. We need each other, but I am willing to look into other options if I have to," Leon insisted.

They stared at each other for a long time, but then a smile finally broke out on Sam's face and he extended his hand.

"That won't be necessary. I can find a way to make it work," he acquiesced and they shook hands.

"Well, with that out of the way we can get on with my plans for what we stole," Leon remarked as he settled into a chair.

"I'm listening," Sam responded as he retrieved some drinks from a cabinet behind his desk.

"We both know it is only a matter of time before the empire comes after us and that we can't defend our current position. They know Altaius is the main pirate holding, and the only reason they haven't wiped you out before now is because they had bigger concerns, but that won't be the case for much longer."

"When do you think they'll come for us?" Sam asked as he settled into the chair behind his desk, having finished pouring the drinks.

"After they finish with the interest. They will need time to increase their forces before attacking another nation, which will be the perfect time to eliminate a minor nuisance such as ourselves."

"Makes sense. So you want to use the building materials we stole to set up a base on another planet?"

"Exactly, except that I don't know of any planets where the empire won't find us. There are a few where we could hide for a while, but they'd find us eventually."

A secretive smile spread across Sam's face and he began going through his desk drawers while Leon watched with some confusion.

"Don't tell me you actually know somewhere we can go?"

"I was able to hide from the union long enough to get them to lose interest in me after deserting, wasn't I?" Sam responded without pausing in his search.

Finally finding what he was looking for, he pulled out a rolled up sheet of paper and placed it in front of his brother.

"More paper," Leon grunted as he unrolled it to find a crudely sketched map.

"Yeah. No matter how much technology we have, the stuff always seems to hang around," Sam commented as he closed the drawers and came around the desk to stand beside Leon.

Around the edges of the map were systems Leon knew well, but the center was mostly blank save for a single unnamed dot near the center. The empty space was filled with distance and orbit calculations leading to the dot from each of the neighboring stars.

"Okay, what is this?"

"I figured the police wouldn't follow me into a void, and I had a few days of food and water on my ship, so I decided to hide in this one until my trail went cold. But while I was flying around to occupy my time, I came across a planet all by itself out there. No star or any other planets."

"A rogue planet?"

"Yes, but this one actually had an atmosphere with some plant and animal life, which I later found out was owed to an active core and a moon to help keep it stable. There wasn't much, but it was enough to survive on. I landed, built myself a shelter, and stayed a couple months until I figured they had given up on me. There wasn't anywhere else to go, so I came here, but I made sure I could find my way back again. You never know when you need a good hideout."

"Sounds perfect. Let's get the supplies and get out there!" Leon exclaimed, rolling up the map as he stood and headed for the door.

He waited there impatiently as Sam calmly finished his drink before deigning to follow him.

OES Dragon's Breath
2:16 P.M.

"Tell me everything," Canza ordered the pilot sitting across from him in the dreadnaught's conference room. Secondary Farra had finally joined him for the campaign and had already debriefed the survivors of the pirate attack. He claimed this one witnessed something important.

"This isn't the first time my convoy has been attacked by pirates, and at first this didn't seem any different from before. They were waiting for us at the border of the Hyperspace Vortex and attacked as soon as we dropped to normal space. Our escort reacted instantly, but somehow the pirates managed to take them out and disable us before we could turn around and jump back to hyperspace," she began.

"You didn't notice anything new in their tactics?" Canza asked.

"Only that they were careful to disable as many of our fighters as possible instead of destroying them outright. They later retrieved the pilots and transferred them to one of our transports before leaving."

"You're saying they avoided killing anyone?" Canza clarified, and she replied in the affirmative.

He was careful not to let his surprise show to the others, but this was a shocking piece of information. It wasn't unusual for pirates to leave people alive, but it wasn't normal for them to go through this much trouble to ensure the safety of their victims.

"Continue."

"They boarded us and began transferring the supplies to their own ship, and a couple of them found me in the cockpit. One of them attacked me, but an officer came in and stopped him before he could do much. Then he got another pirate to help him pull both of them out of there."

Farra looked at him as if he'd just revealed a great secret, but Canza just shot him an annoyed look in response. The report was incredible, but officers of their rank should maintain composure at all times.

"So even pirates frown upon someone behaving like an animal," Canza mused, then asked her if there was anything else.

"Many of them were wearing masks, and the one who stopped the attack on me spoke in a Vehlan accent."

"Were any of them not wearing masks?" Farra questioned.

"Yes, sir. There appeared to be two separate factions. One with the masks who behaved like disciplined troops, and one without the masks that acted like typical ruffians."

"Thank you, Pilot. Your powers of observation allowed you to bring us some crucial information. I am granting you two weeks leave as a reward for this service. Dismissed," Canza concluded, then she stood up, saluted, and left the room.

"The masked pirates must be enemy soldiers who escaped Vehla who decided to sign on with the pirates," Farra commented.

"That was to be expected. They held out for a long time, and such people aren't likely to submit even after being defeated. With nowhere else to go, a life of crime quickly becomes the best, if not only, option."

"I don't understand why they would wear masks. One way or the other we know who they are and will be coming for them, so what purpose does it serve to conceal their identity on a raid."

"Perhaps they still hope to return to a normal life one day, and hope to hide any crimes they commit until then."

"Joining the pirates also gives them a chance to continue fighting us."

"Yes, but they still aren't a threat. We'll deal with all the pirates once we're finished with the Merchant's Interest. It's time they were dealt with anyway," Canza stated.

They left the conference room and went to the tactical room to begin planning for a strike on Altaius. The first thing Canza did was search for anyone within their fleet with experience fighting pirates, and he did not come up empty.

"Have Captain Zenzal of the Thunderstrike report to me immediately," he ordered the bridge.

OES Dragon's Breath
2:57 P.M.

"Captain Alvise Zenzal reporting as ordered, sir," Zenzal announced with a salute.

"At ease, Captain. I understand you have some experience fighting pirates?" Primary Canza responded.

"That's correct, sir. Five years ago the Thunderstrike was deployed into the Outer Territories near the Magnin border to drive out the pirates who had established themselves there."

"Read this report and tell me your impressions."

He activated his palco and brought up the report the primary sent from his own and read through the pilot's report, growing concerned as he did so.

"This troubles you?" Canza observed after he finished.

"Yes, sir, it does. What I just read tells me the pirates are the most powerful they have ever been."

"Explain."

"The fact that all the pirates are based on a single planet leads most people to believe they function as a single organization, but this is a misconception. They are split into several different factions with little to no cooperation between them, and each one is led by its own captain."

"You think that has changed?"

"The pilot reported overhearing the mission commander accuse her attacker of having formerly worked for Black Tempest. Traditionally, the factions are designated by color, with black being among the most powerful. This interaction tells me that they were taken over by another faction, and if a captain was able to do that, it stands to reason he would use that power to force all the factions to submit to his command, unifying them for the first time in history."

"You aren't suggesting they're a legitimate threat!" Secondary Farra exclaimed, causing Zenzal to notice him for the first time.

He felt instant disdain for the man, feeling he was unworthy of the position. From what Zenzal knew of him, he'd never had an original thought in his life and never acted without precise orders from his superiors.

"Not an existential threat, no, but with our new campaign we will be moving a lot of supplies. Combined with the fact they've been joined by ex-union soldiers who almost certainly know our supply routes, they can cause us costly delays," the captain responded, careful not to let his dislike show.

“They won't be any kind of threat for long. Dismissed, Captain,” Canza concluded, and Zenzal saluted before departing to return to his ship.

Once back, he would begin making his own plans for defending against the pirates, and maybe even destroying them. He liked what he saw in Primary Canza so far, but knew Farra wasn't going to take this seriously, and as such felt that he should.

Chapter Fifteen
Epiphany

OES Dragon's Breath
Saturday, January 25th, 2708
11:23 A.M.

"All bomber squadrons, target and destroy the defense grid," Canza ordered.

"Defense grids are meant to supplement a fleet and can do little on their own. Why would they remove their ships but leave it active?" Farra questioned.

"To force us to destroy it so we can't appropriate it, and to cause us as much trouble as possible," Canza sighed.

He kept careful watch for any traps as his bombers blasted the satellites, then ordered the rest of his fleet to assume orbit once the path was clear.

"Status of ground defenses?"

"All military bases appear to be abandoned, but automatic defenses register as active, including interceptors."

"A heavy enough barrage should be enough to destroy them without risking our people," Farra suggested.

"No. We've wasted enough ordnance. Show me a tactical scan of the planetary capital," Canza disagreed. The requested display appeared on the main screen showing buildings in grid format and the people within as small dots.

"I suppose we could always take the cities and ignore the bases," Farra mused.

"You need to learn how to think like the enemy, Farra. It is not enough for them to simply inconvenience us. We can't see them, but their soldiers are still there."

The primary focused on the display while using the controls on the arm of his chair to manipulate the image. He zoomed in on a section tightly packed with buildings, then zeroed in on a high-rise filled to capacity with people and tagged it for Tactical.

"Destroy that building," he ordered.

"Minimize collateral damage, sir?"

"Negative."

"Understood. Firing."

"Main screen to visual."

They didn't see anything for nearly two minutes, but then their missile struck and the building exploded into a massive fireball. The shockwave collapsed the two neighboring buildings and debris shredded the rest, igniting fires wherever it landed.

He watched as people poured out of the surviving buildings and ran as fast as they could away from the scene. Emergency crews eventually arrived and worked to contain the destruction and panic, all in vain as evidenced when a burning building collapsed into itself.

Once the full-effect was achieved, the primary ordered Communications to open a general channel to be received around the planet.

"This is Primary Max Canza of the Ordeon Empire. It is obvious to me there are still Vehlans on this planet preparing for an insurgency, and I will not tolerate this. If you do not deactivate the automatic weapons on your bases and surrender yourselves within the next five minutes, I will begin a full-scale bombardment, starting with the heaviest population centers."

He ordered the channel cut, then leaned back in his chair.

"I expected you to order a nuclear strike on the city," Farra commented.

"This delivers the same message while keeping the city intact so there is minimal impact on their economy. That economy is our primary goal, but I will burn this entire planet if I have to, and now they know it."

"Surrender signal coming in now, sir," Communications reported.

"Automatic defenses are powering down, sir," Tactical confirmed.

"Send in the invasion force," Canza ordered, then waited a moment as the order was carried out and their transports headed for the planet.

"All should be standard procedure from here. Come get some lunch with me," he remarked to Farra, then stood and went to the elevator, but paused before entering.

"Send rescue teams to the bomb site."

Troop Transport
12:11 P.M.

About time, Private Menza thought to himself as the lights turned orange and he stood up in unison with the others.

"Change of plans. Primary Canza scared them into surrendering, so we aren't going to be doing any fighting," Lieutenant Hancen announced, eliciting disappointed groans from Menza and others. They were looking forward to crushing their enemy, but they quickly fell silent to dutifully listen to the new orders.

"Each squad will be assigned to a rescue team evacuating the area around the building Canza bombed. Your job is to provide cover, but you are to do so with minimum necessary force. We have shown them our strength, now it is time to show them our mercy," Hancen explained.

A buzzer sounded to signal successful atmospheric insertion and the soldiers lined up behind the doors. Menza's squad was exiting via the main ramp at the rear of the craft along with another squad, but the rest would leave through other doors placed all around the passenger section.

The transport slowed, all the doors flew open and the soldiers jumped out onto the rooftop two meters below then ran to the center where they met up with the rescue teams.

Thick, black smoke poured out of the building beneath them, and Menza thought he felt a rumble as if from something collapsing inside, but he put all this out of his mind and focused on the task ahead. His helmet was capable of filtering out the smoke, and his armor also contained an independent air supply if that should fail to be enough.

The officers assigned each soldier to a rescuer, then they descended into the structure, splitting up as needed to search room by room. Thermal detectors in their helmets helped speed the search, but only in areas far enough from the fires, which wasn't many.

None of the occupants resisted as they were simply glad for the rescue, regardless of who was doing the rescuing, so the soldiers paid less attention to defense and more to helping in the effort.

As they went through each floor, the transports hovered outside any openings they could find, or made one if necessary, and took the victims onboard.

Halfway through the fourth floor down, with thirty-one left to go, the building shook violently, and everyone froze in their tracks as if afraid any movement would send it all crashing down.

"All teams, exfil immediately!" Hancen ordered over comms, and Menza was only too happy to obey.

He followed three others to the nearest pick up point and was about to enter the room behind them when he heard faint crying. Pausing in the doorway, he considered ignoring it, but then chided himself for being a coward and went back into the hallway to track the source.

An anguished scream tore through the sounds of the building falling apart, and he ran towards it, soon drawing near enough to still hear it when the scream faded back into crying.

He burst through a door to find himself in a residence that faced the building destroyed in the attack. Debris had torn through the walls, and one piece had also taken out a support column causing the floor above to collapse.

Amidst all of this was a little girl, no more than eight years old, with her arms wrapped around a dead man and her face buried in his chest. When he moved closer, Menza saw a piece of shrapnel buried in the man's forehead above his eyes blankly staring at the ceiling.

"Private Menza! Report!" Sergeant Lancia shouted via his comm unit.

"I found a little girl, sir. I'm getting her out now," he responded, surprised at his own calmness.

"Get moving! Structural scans indicate the building is in imminent danger of collapse!"

That got him moving.

He rushed up to the girl and reached out to grab her, but before he could get close enough, she looked up at him, screamed, and scurried into a corner behind a couch, or what was left of a couch.

"I'm not going to hurt you. I'm here to help," he tried reassuring her, but she just screamed again, then started choking on the thickening smoke.

He couldn't understand how she could be more scared of him than the situation, but another coughing fit on her part reminded him he was wearing a helmet and her fear was probably caused by not being able to see his face.

He took a deep breath, held it, then removed the helmet and knelt down to look her in the face. She finally stopped screaming, or trying to scream, and stared at him wide-eyed. He held the helmet out towards her, then grabbed her by the wrist and pulled her out when she reached for it.

She struggled against him, but he held her tight in one arm while he placed the helmet on her head so she could use the filtration system, but of course it was too big for her and smoke continued to flow in from underneath. There was a blanket on the couch, so he grabbed it and shoved it under the helmet to create a makeshift seal, then he gripped her in both arms and ran back into the hallway.

The floor had a few new holes in it, but he ran around them just like on an obstacle course. His lungs felt like they were about to burst, but he continued to hold his breath.

When he found the exfil point again, he saw his transport still hovering outside the window, so he put on a burst of speed and jumped into the back, falling onto his side. Someone took the girl from him as he finally let out his breath in a coughing fit, after which he rolled onto his back to see Lancia staring at the building receding behind them.

"What genius said that place was about to fall?" he asked in an irritated tone.

Before anyone could respond, the high-rise collapsed in upon itself, spewing a cloud of dust into the air.

Triage Zone
2:21 P.M.

Deep in thought, Private Menza sat on the rear bumper of a combat jeep watching the continuing activity around him. The doctors had checked him for smoke inhalation or injury, but had found nothing. His squad was in the process of turning over its duties to a fresh unit, so he had some time to himself.

He saw Ordonians working side by side with Merchants, and even a few Vehlans, to extinguish the remaining fires and aid the injured. Nobody was fighting, or even arguing, but all were focused on the task at hand.

The conquerors working with the conquered.

"There you are," someone said, and he looked up to see Sergeant Lancia walking towards him. He started to stand to attention, but the NCO waved a hand to tell him to stay seated.

"How's the girl?" Menza asked.

"She inhaled plenty of smoke, but she will recover. I'm more curious about what's on your mind that's so important you needed to sit here by yourself."

"It's nothing, Sergeant. What are my orders?"

"Your orders are to tell me what you're thinking."

The private sighed and looked away. He wasn't sure he could put his thoughts and feelings into words for himself, much less his superior.

"I've always believed we were to show no mercy to our enemies. Anyone who would stand in the way of progress deserves to die, and what the empire has to offer is worth more than the lives of a few fools. Then today..."

"Then today you are being ordered into a burning building to save the lives of those fools, and even when you are ordered out, you find yourself going back in to save one more."

"I don't understand it."

"You haven't been a soldier for very long, and today you learned one of the most important lessons of this life. They may be our enemies, and fools, but they are still people who suffer every time we fire our weapons."

"That doesn't matter. We offer a better future, but they do everything in their power to stop us."

"It does matter. We will do what we have to do to create the future our people have worked so long to achieve, but that will only happen if we offer peace and mercy in equal measure to the war and suffering."

"I'm not sure I understand."

He had continued to observe the relief efforts through the conversation, but now Lancia handed something over to him and he looked down to see his helmet which he had inadvertently left with the girl.

"None of us really do. All we can be certain about is the empire and the future we seek to create. The rest is for others to figure out," Lancia concluded, then stood and ordered him to report back to the transport before walking off.

He stood up to follow, but before he did, he donned the helmet and found within it a whole new perspective.

It is a soldier's job to kill, but it is also a soldier's job to heal.

Rogue Planet
6:21 P.M.

"I still can't believe a planet like this exists," Leon commented after disembarking from the small yacht.

It was dark, but his genetically altered eyes adjusted quickly, allowing him to see a forest lit with a dull yellow glow.

"You can't see them from here, but that glow comes from natural crystal formations. All the plant life here clusters around those formations," Sam explained.

"Which explains how there can be life without sunlight," Leon responded, then he turned to look in the other direction where he saw only bare ground.

"This way," Sam prodded, then led him to the other side of the yacht where there was a small dwelling crudely constructed from wood.

"Are there enough plants and animals to support a population?" Leon asked as they entered the shelter.

"Not for long, but it should be long enough for us to get farm operations running and we can always bring in additional supplies."

"I want to minimize travel to and from this planet as much as possible, so supply runs are going to be few and far between."

There were only two rooms in the shelter, a bedroom and a main room. In the center of the main room was a lopsided wooden table with a relatively straight chair, then there was a long bench next to a wall and in another corner sat a box full of paper documents.

"Why didn't you use your palco?" Leon asked.

"I disabled it after deserting so it couldn't be tracked, and only started using it again after reaching Altaius and someone helped me to secure the network."

"So where did you get all the paper?"

"From the logbook on the ship I stole."

"What logbook? Logs are digitally recorded, like everything else."

"All ships have a hardcopy in case of emergency. If the digital log is inoperable, or the ship is completely without power, the crew can document their repair attempts and possibly leave a final message. Didn't you know that?" Sam answered, and Leon merely shook his head in response.

"Infantry man to the last, I see," Sam joked, then picked up the box and set it on the table, careful to place it so it wouldn't slide off.

"What is all of this?" Leon questioned as he pulled out a few papers and glanced at them.

"I had to do something to pass the time, so I surveyed the planet. Good thing I did too, because that saves us the effort of having to find a location for our new base," Sam responded, then placed a map on the table and pointed at a spot.

"You want to build in a canyon?"

"That's right. The river is much smaller than it used to be, providing us with plenty of room on either side. It's hidden, defensible, and provides us with plenty of fresh water."

He pulled out another paper, this one a detailed survey of the canyon in question. Leon studied it and the larger map, and quickly decided his brother was right.

"Let's use the ship to get some detailed scans for the engineers then get back to Altaius. We can discuss the logistics of keeping this place secret during the trip."

Chapter Sixteen
Hostile Takeover

Merchanta
OES Dragon's Breath
Tuesday, February 4th, 2708
8:30 A.M.

The homeworld of the Merchant's Interest appeared on the main screen, little more than a large dot from the fleet's position on the edge of the solar system.

"Enlarge," Primary Canza ordered, and the dot was replaced with a planet surrounded with thousands of ships, satellites, and space stations.

"Not all of those ships are Vehlan," Secondary Farra observed.

"The rest are private security employed by the corporations," Canza explained.

"They must have waited until now because they actually thought the Vehlans alone were enough to stop us," Farra suggested.

The primary studied the planet's defenses on both the visual and tactical views, then made some small adjustments to his strategy. The additional defenders posed no threat, but that was no reason to be overconfident.

"Wave one, commence."

Four H-shaped imperial carriers appeared on either side of the planet and launched their fighters which proceeded towards the planet at full speed while eight cruisers with semi-circular bows and triangular sterns stayed with the carriers.

The defenders redeployed most of their ships in the threatened sectors to block the fighters, but did not move against the larger ships. Four of the cruisers moved forward to provide cover fire while the fighters fought to break through the blockade.

"Wave two, commence."

On either side of the carrier groups, an Ordonian dreadnaught escorted by two destroyers popped out of hyperspace and charged the weakened sections of the blockade, firing as they went. They easily destroyed their targets, then turned to assist the first wave.

Dozens of troop transports launched from the carriers and flew through the gaps in the defensive line before they could be closed.

"Main fleet, advance."

The rest of the imperial fleet headed by the dreadnaught Dragon's Breath fired up its engines and moved towards the planet at half-speed. Several defenders fled into hyperspace at the sight of them, but Canza paid them no mind. It was possible they intended to outflank him, but it was more likely they were running for their lives, and they posed no danger regardless.

"Fire at will," he ordered the moment they were in range.

His ships spread around the planet like a horde of insects, decimating the defenses while receiving few casualties of their own. The remaining nine-tenths of the defenders chose to surrender rather than be destroyed, and were escorted away from the battle area while the main imperial feet assumed bombardment positions.

"Nuclear missile armed. Targeting the capital city."

"I did not give that order," Canza rebuked, causing everyone present to look at him in surprise.

"Didn't the emperor decree that Nuclear Coup be standard policy after Vehla?" Farra questioned, referring to the imperial strategy where they used a nuclear weapon to destroy an enemy's capital city upon achieving orbital control over their homeworld.

"Yes, he did, but that doesn't apply here. Destroying the capital will wreck the economy beyond repair, and we need it intact for the next phase. Target the city Pena's Retreat."

His studies of the planet had revealed this particular city to be nothing but a resort where the richest business owners could purchase property and live isolated from the rest of the nation. It was almost entirely self-sustaining, making little difference on the economy at large.

The secondary hesitated, unsure whether he should follow the orders of his emperor or those of his immediate superior, but then he confirmed the order for Tactical.

"Target locked. Firing."

They watched as the missile disappeared from their view then was replaced by a mushroom cloud on the planet's surface.

"Target destroyed."

"Deploy ground invasion."

Merchanta
9:13 A.M.

The sounds of battle assaulted Menza's senses as soon as the doors opened, and he gripped his rifle tight as he ran down a side ramp with the rest of his squad.

Three gunships blasted past them, fired rockets, then climbed back into the sky, but not before one was shot up by a laser turret. Black smoke poured out of its starboard engine, but it still managed to get away.

A line of tanks pounded the enemy base with heavy weapons, which responded with artillery fire of its own. Interceptor weaponry on both sides stopped most of the shots, but plenty still made it through.

Barrier drones, which were nothing more than motorized barricades, formed up several yards behind the tanks, and the infantry took cover behind them, Menza's squad included. They would wait here until the big guns could create a hole in the enemy defenses.

"Why didn't we just drop into the base?" a soldier in Menza's squad wondered aloud.

"This isn't a base, it's a vault. It has all the defenses money can buy, including a shield," their corporal responded.

"That also explains why it's in the middle of nowhere," another soldier grumbled as he glanced back at the thick woods behind their transports.

Their tanks pelted the enemy shield continuously, and the defenders kept firing back, but they were easily able to hear each other thanks to their helmet comms.

"I'm surprised the Merchants would allow the Vehlans anywhere near one of their vaults, much less have them defend it," Menza commented.

"Those fleeing Union space probably took over the best bases for themselves."

An electric crackling noise washed over them, and the sounds of explosions coming from the base changed to include that of rending metal and shattering carbocrete.

A formation of bombers shot over them, and the soldiers instinctively covered their heads as the ground shook beneath them. When they looked up again, a cloud of black smoke was rising up to obscure the clear blue sky.

The tanks finally rumbled forward, firing as they went, and the barrier drones followed with the soldiers directly behind marching in the undisturbed ground between tread grooves.

Then the tanks suddenly veered to the side and the drones surged forward with the soldiers keeping pace behind them. The tanks ceased firing with their main cannons, but continued to cover the infantry's advance with their smaller, rapid-fire weapons.

The drones rolled through the gaps in the base wall, their treads crushing the rubble into gravel beneath them, then continued forward several meters before stopping to form a solid barrier again. Soldiers rushed in behind them and set up medic stations, platoon command posts, and ammo crates.

"Our orders are to proceed directly to the center of the base to assist in securing the command center. Any resistance will be dealt with as needed, but we won't be stopping to secure anything until we reach the center. Move out!" Menza's lieutenant briefed them via helmet comms.

Every fifth drone swung back and to the right, creating gaps in the wall through which the fully armored soldiers ran through in staggered formation up to ten at a time.

They found themselves on a small street with featureless buildings on each side, and quickly spread out to cover both sides and the middle in a staggered formation. Menza ended up on the right side, but soon realized he didn't have much more cover than those out in the street.

Almost immediately, several grenades came flying through the air and landed among them. Those who were close enough either kicked them or scooped them up to throw back while everyone else dove to the ground and covered their heads, and Menza was in the latter group.

Not all were fast enough in getting rid of the grenades, and a few went off in their midst. Screams filled the air as Menza crawled as fast as he could to a nearby doorway where he then stood and pressed flat against the door.

Then the shooting started.

Red lasers and white plasma filled the air while medics crawled through the street, moving from one casualty to the next. A couple soldiers helped to move the wounded to safety, but most were laying down cover fire.

"Can anyone see where they are?"

"Just fire along the path of their lasers!"

"It's not having any effect!"

The shouts of his platoon broke through the shock of having been nearly blown up, so Menza took a deep breath, then stuck his head out to take a look.

He spotted several Vehlans behind makeshift barricades in the nearby intersection and saw some more firing from the second floor of the buildings on the other side, then pulled back into cover just before a laser bolt shot through where his head had been a moment before.

"I see them, Sergeant," he radioed to Lancia, then signaled the enemy's precise position using the controls in the fingertips of his gloves. Lancia confirmed the report, then transmitted the data to the whole platoon so it appeared on their HUDs.

They concentrated their firepower on the barricades, which began to fall apart under the barrage. One Vehlan panicked and made a run for it, but Menza shot him before he could get far.

The laser fire tapered off, allowing an Ordonian to pop out of cover long enough to throw a grenade. It landed between the barricades and exploded, sending bodies flying in all directions.

The remaining defenders ran for it, and the Ordonians were ordered to give chase.

They ran through the intersection, firing at the retreating defenders. Menza saw one duck into an alleyway and broke from the group to pursue him.

He nearly had his target when someone else burst out a side door and slammed him against the opposite wall. He pushed his assailant off and spun around with his rifle up and prepared to fire, but stopped when he saw there were four of them with their own weapons pointed at him.

There was no way he could take them all out, so he lowered his rifle just enough to point at the ground hoping it would be enough to placate them into not shooting him.

"You've already lost, so surrender now and get it over with," he admonished. One snorted derisively while two of the others stared at him angrily, but the fourth looked unsure of himself.

“Typical Imp arrogance. You're surrounded and outnumbered, yet you're demanding our surrender?” the snorter accused.

“You can kill me, yes, but what good would it do you but make your own deaths more likely? If you surrender, you will live.”

“Maybe we should listen to him?” the younger soldier suggested, still slightly out of breath.

“You want to just give up? You want to let them get away with everything they've done? You want the union to remain enslaved?”

“N-n-no.”

“Then shut up.”

“Why don't we just shoot him and get it over with?” a third one suggested.

“We might be able to use him to get out of here. Even if we can't, I want to take the time to enjoy his death.”

A pair of Ordonians appeared at the alleyway entrance and took aim. Menza saw them and dove to his left, taking the younger Vehlan to the ground with him.

He waited for the shooting to stop, then rolled onto his back to see his people walking up and got back on his feet.

“Do you still want to surrender?” he asked the enemy soldier. Frightened, he only managed to nod his consent.

“Keep this up, Menza, and people are going to start thinking you're soft.”

“One less person is dead right now, so it really doesn't matter what people think,” Menza responded as he helped his prisoner up and disarmed him.

“He's a Nihl! His death would be a public service.”

“Possibly. It's also possible he will become a productive citizen of the empire. Now we have the chance to find out.”

Revenue Central

3:42 P.M.

The transport door opened and twelve armored soldiers hustled down the ramp to form an honor guard from its bottom to the steps of the Merchant's capitol building.

Smoke could still be seen rising into the overcast sky as Canza walked down the ramp, but all was silent. There were no sounds of battle as there was no one left in the city to fight.

On the primary's left was Secondary Farra while on his right walked Knight Captain Bazaine, the one who would be overseeing the assimilation of the Merchant's Interest into the empire. For once, Canza didn't care that a Star Knight was taking a job that would normally be his. The interest was set up more along the lines of a corporation than a government, and he had no desire to be involved with the world of business.

They ascended the steps to the capitol's entrance at the top of which waited four men and two women in expensive suits, the nation's top leaders. Four Ordonian soldiers stood guard around them.

"You are conquered, Chairman. Surrender control of your remaining territories and submit to the authority of the Ordeon Empire," Canza told the gray-haired man in the group's center.

"We are prepared to surrender at this time, Primary. The Vehlans promised to stop you, but they have failed. All the necessary documents have already been drawn up, so if you will come inside we can put an end to all of this."

"It was clear long before now that the Vehlans were incapable of stopping us. You could have prevented much loss of life if you had surrendered earlier, so why wait until now?" Farra questioned as they headed inside.

"Pure self-interest mingled with foolish hope. We want to remain independent, so we held out as long as possible hoping to find a way to do so. But any good businessman knows when to cut his losses, and that's where we find ourselves now."

"Chairman, I am Knight Captain Bazaine. The emperor sent me to integrate your assets into the empire."

"How will you be doing that?"

"I will restructure your businesses to be compliant with imperial law while maintaining productivity."

"That will be more difficult than you think."

"We will see."

Chapter Seventeen
Transitions

Rogue Planet (New Hope)
Wednesday, February 5th, 2708
9:04 A.M.

Hands clasped behind his back, Colonel Tyquese stood at the window in his freshly completed office carved into the stone and peered out at the canyon below past the reflection of his dark-skinned face. Harvested crystals cast a dim yellow glow on the structures dotting the canyon floor, sparing them the power expense of artificial lighting.

The river which had formed the canyon was much smaller now than in the distant past, leaving a considerable amount of space on either side and almost no danger of flooding.

Most of that space was dedicated to farms which they had constructed inside large barns to grant them environmental control which would lead to greater crop yields. An outdoor recreation and exercise area sat halfway between the canyon's east wall and the river.

At the base's south end resided the prefabricated structures they'd stolen from the imperials which served as either barracks or armories. A metal bridge connected that section to the canyon's other side where all their vehicles were stored in a hastily dug alcove.

For added security, he'd ordered the main base built underground within the canyon walls. So far all they had was the command center which included offices and quarters for the higher ranks. It would take more time to finish digging the tunnels and other rooms, but once it was finished, they would move everything but the farms inside where it was safer.

There was no spaceport yet, so ships were simply landing on the ground. The engineers were looking into the possibility of building that underground as well.

While his people worked to build this base, he had sought to strengthen their forces. In a joint raid with Sam's pirates, he had stolen a communications satellite from a small nation and reprogrammed it for secure transmissions. This allowed him to contact a few union ships on their classified frequencies and recruit them to cause.

He hoped there were still more out there, but he didn't know which ones or remember all their frequencies, so he just had to hope they would find each other along the way.

Additionally, he had sent out several squads to secure the equipment he had hidden on different planets and bring it back here. It wasn't enough to bring them to full strength, but it was enough to cause some damage.

His brother had also done well, establishing new pirate bases within several nations, including the Ordeon Empire. When Leon asked how he managed to create a base in their territory without them finding out, Sam had simply told him not to ask such questions.

So far, the other pirate captains weren't causing them any trouble. It probably had something to do with almost all of their raids being successful, building their power and wealth far beyond what it was before, even with the tribute they owed Sam.

"Sir, there is a message for you from Captain Tyquese."

"Put it through," Leon responded, returning to his desk.

No live messages were being transmitted directly to or from this base, but were instead being sent through a series of relay stations before reaching their destination. They weren't taking the chance a signal would get picked up and traced back here.

Empire finished conquest of Interest.
Expect them to come after us next.
Return to Altaius.

-Sam

Revenue Central
Capitol Building
10:03 A.M.

"You can't do this!"

"Never say that to a Star Knight," Bazaine threatened. The chairman glanced at him, then swallowed his frustration and pride before continuing.

"I only mean to say that if you want to benefit from our high GDP, then you need to do things our way."

"I have studied your nation and its economy thoroughly, and I know how to change things without causing damage."

The chairman glanced over the holographic reports hovering over the conference table, but couldn't see how the knight could possibly expect this to work. He wanted them to change their business practices to comply with imperial law, but to do so would practically bankrupt them.

"I understand that being a part of the empire means abiding by your laws, but restrictive government procedures always result in loss of profit. That's exactly why we seceded from the union in the first place."

"They granted your independence so they could benefit from your criminal activities while supposedly keeping their own hands clean. Their willingness to sacrifice their own principles led to their destruction. We refuse to make the same mistake."

"Then you will receive far less than they ever did."

"You are failing to see the opportunities present due to current conditions. The Hundred Years War caused a lot of damage to the Vehlan territories, and many things once easily available to them are now scarce. Land you use to grow drugs can be changed over to grow food which will then supply the areas facing shortages, and you won't have the expense of having to smuggle it in," Bazaine described.

The chairman looked at the reports again, studying them more closely this time in the areas of food and illicit drug production. When he saw that the knight had a point, he looked at the other now illegal enterprises and the suggested conversions.

"If we do things your way, we will remain steady, for now. But when things calm down and the reconstruction is finished, profits will decrease dramatically."

"That will only happen once we have achieved our destiny, and we will no longer need that money."

Altaius
Red Base
7:34 P.M.

"Two beers," Eric requested as he and Jeremy sat on stools at the bar.

"Feeling generous?" Jeremy quipped as he accepted the glass bottle.

"I realized a while ago that I never properly thanked you for saving my life back on Vehla."

"Don't mention it," Jeremy responded, then they clinked their bottles together and took a swig.

"Maybe we'll have a drink back on Vehla one day," Eric commented.

"Well now, haven't you changed. Just a couple weeks ago you thought we were doomed."

"Yes, and I still have a feeling that's the most likely outcome, but I can't deny everything we've accomplished in such a short amount of time. Makes me think there might be a bit of hope after all."

"For a moment there, I thought I'd come in here with the wrong person, but that last statement was just as depressing as it was encouraging, so I know it has to be you," Jeremy joked, and Eric laughed with him.

"Wha' ya doin' here?" someone slurred behind them, and they turned to see five pirates surrounding a pair of Vehlans, a sergeant and a private.

"Same thing as you, having a drink or two," the sergeant responded.

"Na wha' I mean! We be doin' all the wor' while you an' ya pals jes be sittin' aroun'!"

"Red Sam hired us, and it's up to him to decide what we do. If you have a problem with that, take it up with him."

"I thin' ya'll up to sumthin', sumthin' ya ain't tellin' us!"

"Our business is our own, as is yours. Now all we want to do is have a quiet drink after a day's work, so I suggest you leave the thinking to the bigwigs and let us be."

"I don' like ya attitu'e," the pirate threatened, causing Eric and Jeremy to stand up and move a little closer.

The pirates thought they were nothing more than a mercenary company hired by Red Sam to defeat Black Tempest then to help keep the other factions in line. It was surprising a confrontation like this hadn't happened earlier.

"Get away from us!" the Vehlan private yelled and shoved the nearest pirate.

Big mistake.

Two pirates grabbed him and threw him into a table while the others went after the sergeant, but he reacted fast enough to grab one and throw him into the others.

One of those pirates stumbled into Eric and Jeremy, who grabbed him and flipped him over the bar, sending their beers smashing to the floor in the process.

The whole bar erupted into chaos as people from both sides moved in to help the original combatants, or simply targeted someone they didn't like.

Someone punched Eric in the face, knocking him to the floor, but then Jeremy grabbed him and slammed his face on the bar hard enough to knock him out.

"If you keep this up you'll never be able to buy me enough beer to make up for saving your skin," he quipped as he helped up his friend.

He was about to respond with something equally sarcastic, but instead pulled him back in time to avoid being clobbered with a chair before kicking the aggressor in the gut.

"Looks like you owe me one now."

"Let's just call it even."

Time for talking disappeared as the fight grew more and more chaotic and they were forced to focus entirely on surviving it.

Several laser bolts shot into the ceiling, raining dust and debris down on the combatants, shocking them into ceasing the fight and looking towards the entrance.

"Knock it off!" a rifle wielding pirate sergeant demanded. He then calmly looked several people in the eye as he sauntered into the center of the room.

"What is going on here!" Captain Mathison shouted as he burst through the door with several armored Vehlan soldiers trailing him.

A few soldiers attempted to mumble an answer, but he cut them off with a wave of his hand.

"It doesn't matter what happened. That this happened at all is a disgrace. You will clean this up this instant!" he ordered, then turned on one heel and stormed out.

The pirates looked towards their sergeant, who scratched the side of his rifle with his trigger finger as he considered their own punishment.

"All the pirates involved in this idiocy will participate in the next raid, and your loot percentages will go to the bar's owner. Now get out of here."

He stared at them until each and every pirate had gone, then he shot an annoyed look at the Vehlans before leaving himself.

"Still alive?" Jeremy asked from behind Eric, and he turned to look at him only for both of them to bust out laughing. Many of the others did the same.

They were bruised and bloody, but it also felt good to release the tension built up over the last year, especially that from the last couple months.

Red Command Center
Friday, February 7th, 2708
12:04 P.M.

"We need to decide how we're going to stop the Imps from blasting us to pieces," Sam revealed after he and his brother sat down to lunch.

"How long do you think it'll be until they come after us?"

"Couple weeks. They'll want to secure their hold on the interest first, and we can buy more time if necessary with more raids on their supply lines."

"Sounds right. Do you know if they have any idea how many of us soldiers are here?"

"My sources tell me they suspect a few hundred. They know exactly how many are still at large, but believe most have gone their own way."

"That makes things a little easier for us. I'll move all of my people to New Hope along with all of our main operations, and you should do the same for your own operations. The biggest issue is how to make it appear they have eliminated us as a threat once they do come."

"How are we going to do that unless you leave some of your people here for them to find?"

"They only see us as a threat because we're working with you and believe that they will destroy us by cutting off our support, but that still leaves your pirates in danger. Do you have a plan to keep them safe?"

"The ones I want to keep around, yes," Sam responded, causing Leon to pause eating and give him a quizzical look.

"I assume you heard about them nuking a major city on Merchanta?" Sam asked, then continued when his brother nodded in the affirmative. "Well, I think they're going to do the same to one of our bases. If their victory is to look legitimate, that base needs to be fully manned when they do."

The older brother laid his fork on his plate and leaned back in his chair.

"You're talking about condemning hundreds of people to die in a nuclear blast."

"Yes."

"There must be another way."

"The Ordonians are monsters, but they aren't stupid. If they attack and the casualty numbers come up short, they'll know most of us escaped and will come looking."

"You call them monsters, but how are we any different if we do this? We'll be signing their death warrants."

"Those were signed a long time ago."

"What are you talking about?"

"You don't think I'd sacrifice good people like this, do you? I've researched the background of every pirate and personally selected ones who have committed crimes warranting the death penalty in any respectable nation."

Leon leaned forward and asked him to explain his plan. He still appeared uncomfortable, but at least he was listening.

"A man in the black faction has been consolidating power and setting himself up to take charge. Sooner or later he will move against me, and now that he knows what he's up against there is every chance he will succeed, so I need to get rid of him before that happens. To that end, I've decided to grant him the captaincy of the black faction and return Black Base to them. Your upgrades make it a prime target for this nuclear attack, so we will solve two problems for the price of one," he outlined.

The colonel pushed away from the table and began pacing behind his chair.

"And these people are the worst of the worst, even by pirate standards, correct?" he questioned.

"That's right."

"There will need to be another faction here to pad the numbers."

"That will be the yellows. They're cowards, and will surrender as soon as the others are destroyed," Sam told him, then sipped his juice while watching his brother continue to pace.

He finally stopped, then leaned on the back of his chair with a sigh.

"You're right. It's the only way. I'll get my people out of the base," he acquiesced, then turned to head for the door.

"There's one more thing."

"What's that?" Leon asked, and turned to face him again.

"There was an incident the other day between some of your soldiers and my pirates. Apparently, the pirates are growing suspicious of your true identity and motives. I don't think they're going to fall for the hired gun story for much longer."

"We can't tell them who we really are."

"I'm not sure we have a choice."

"You're not seriously suggesting I trust them!"

"No, I'm suggesting you trust me. I know what I'm doing here."

"They'll sell us out to the Ordonians!"

"A few will try, but the captains will want to stay away from the empire even more than they'll want to get rid of us, and they'll keep their people in line."

"How can you be so sure of that?"

"Ordeos doesn't make deals with criminals, so anyone who goes to them will be arrested along with anyone they rat out. Every pirate desires power and wealth, but freedom is far more important."

"Good point. Alright, I'll trust you. I just hope you're right."

Resistance Base
Meeting Hall
7:00 P.M.

Every seat in the auditorium was occupied by a pirate, and even more stood in the aisles and around the walls. Vehlan soldiers in their dark green armor and armed with pistols and knives stood in key positions around the room, placed there by Leon to keep an eye on their less disciplined allies.

As he watched the assembly from his position on the stage beside Sam, Leon continued to wonder if they were making a fatal mistake. Each faction had sent representatives to hear for themselves what the brothers had to say, turning the room into a colorful mosaic with their armbands. The captains and the rest of their personnel watched on monitors from their bases around the planet.

The attendees from the black faction had placed themselves at the very front, but for the moment weren't behaving any more aggressively than the others. Two rows of reds armed with rifles stood between the crowd and the stage.

"I already told my own officers the announcement we're making tonight. If anything happens, they'll fight with us," Sam whispered to Leon as he headed to the podium.

The colonel nodded but kept a wary gaze on the crowd while also choosing to trust his brother. After all, he wouldn't be alive right now if he didn't know how to deal with these crooks. At least that's what he kept telling himself.

"I have become aware of increasing tensions between you and my mercenaries and I realize that I cannot continue lying to you. Our goals can only be achieved if you know the truth, so that is what we have come to tell you," Sam introduced, then stepped aside for Leon to take his place.

"My name is Colonel Leon Tyquese, and I command what is left of the Vehlan Union military. We told you that we are nothing but a mercenary company hired by Red Sam to fight his enemies, but the truth is we continue to serve as soldiers fighting for the union cause."

Utter and complete silence answered him. He looked into their faces, but saw neither shock nor anger. They didn't care who he was, and merely awaited the rest of the story.

"We lost our home, but not our determination to fight for what is right. With nowhere else to go, I came to my brother to seek his help in building a resistance movement against the Ordonians, and he agreed to give that help in return for certain concessions."

This time the crowd shot to its feet and erupted into shouting.

"You've drafted us!"

"I came here to get away from your war!"

"Freedom, not war!"

"You used me to strike at my own people!"

The Vehlan guards tensed up and reached for their weapons, but Leon waved a hand to signal them to stand down. When the shouting continued, Sam stepped up and banged a fist on the podium. The microphone amplified the sound above that of the crowd, and they finally quieted down, but all remained standing.

"You are pirates, not soldiers. That has not changed. Your orders come from Red Sam, and I have no authority over you. This is an alliance, not a conscription," Leon reassured them.

"Not all of us are Vehlans! Why should we support your cause, especially if it means fighting our own people?" someone shouted, and murmurs of consent rippled through the crowd.

This time Sam pushed Leon aside to answer the challenge himself.

"Since when do any of you owe loyalty to any nation? They condemn us as criminals for seeking to live our own lives, and would gladly imprison or execute us given the chance."

"That doesn't mean we want to fight and kill our own people!"

"How many have you killed to steal their stuff? It's okay when it makes you money, but when it's for a cause you suddenly get a guilty conscience?"

No one responded to that, and Sam stepped back to let Leon speak again.

"You are right to ask why you should support our cause. There are many deserters among you who lost faith in the union government and hope for the cause. Why come back to it now?"

He paused to look over the crowd, specifically finding the dark-skinned faces similar to his own and peering into their eyes, daring them to reexamine why they were here.

"Why continue to fight when all hope seems lost? I have asked myself that question, and have concluded there is always hope as long as there are people willing to take a stand. We don't fight for any particular government. We fight for what we believe, and we believe in freedom and justice. Those things are worth fighting for, no matter what."

Soft-rustling filled the room as many sat down again, unable to hold on to their anger when faced with the truth of his words.

"That still doesn't explain what we're getting out of this deal," someone spoke up.

Sam moved up to take over again, but Leon held up a hand to stop him.

"You will continue to receive payment and bonuses per your agreements with your captains. Also, when the union is restored, you will be granted amnesty for all crimes committed in the past and up to the point the legal system is reestablished. Many of you are here only because you had nowhere else to go. This is your chance to make a fresh start."

There was a small scuffle near the middle of the room as a pirate previously standing in the aisle shoved aside someone who still refused to sit and took his seat for himself, and almost all the rest resumed their seats as well.

A gentle hand on his shoulder caused Leon to look back at Sam, who smiled and nodded at him to say he would take it from here.

"I am one of those deserters the colonel mentioned. I'm still not sure I believe the union is anything worth restoring, nor can I say I'm overjoyed to have to put up with my brother again," he started out, receiving a few laughs at the last part. Even Leon allowed himself a small smile.

"That being said, as a pirate, I take an opportunity when I see it. I did that by agreeing to help him in return for his help in destroying Black Tempest, and I continue doing that by using his knowledge of Ordonian and Vehlan operations to make me rich and powerful. Now I see the opportunity to live the life I have always desired, and I'm going to take that one too. Who's with me?"

Nothing but silence answered him.

Nobody spoke for so long that Leon became sure they had failed.

Then someone started clapping, and another followed suit. Soon everyone was on their feet again, but this time in applause, not anger.

Leon's palco vibrated, so he held up his palm and brought up the holographic display at the same time Sam activated his own. He skimmed the report from Captain Mathison, then glanced at his brother to see him smiling. They'd both received the same message.

The pirates had pledged themselves to the cause.

"Now, there are a couple details to sort out. The colonel and I have set up a new headquarters on another planet and will be heading there soon with most of our people. In exchange for the loyalty they have shown, I am returning this base to the Black Faction. It's also time they received a new captain. Pinal Mancini, come up here," Sam continued.

A muscular man stepped out from the group in front and ascended the steps to the stage to the applause of his colleagues, but Leon noticed the others suddenly grow uncomfortable.

"You have demonstrated yourself to be a capable leader, so I name you Black Pinal," Sam announced, then pulled the black band off Pinal's right arm with his left hand while holding something out to him in his right.

The new captain smiled wide, took the object from Sam's hand, and pinned it to his collar, revealing it to be a black skull and crossbones pin similar to the red one on Sam's collar.

"I am placing you in command of Altaius in my absence. Yellow Acker will act as your second-in-command. Continue the raids on Ordonian targets and work on improving our defenses here. They'll be coming for us eventually."

Confused murmurs spread through the crowd as the captains shook hands. From their perspective, Sam was as good as committing suicide, but they also knew he couldn't be that stupid.

Which of course he wasn't, and they would understand what was happening soon enough.

Black Command Center
Monday, February 10th, 2708
3:03 P.M.

"What are you working on in here?" Red Sam asked as he casually stepped into Black Pinal's office.

"Plans to further our mutual interests, of course," Pinal responded, and Sam pretended not to notice how quickly he closed out a program on his desk.

"I assume those plans include the defense of this planet?"

"Of course."

"Good. Tell me what you have in mind," Sam requested, then walked around to view the changes made since the new captain moved in a couple days ago.

"We'll plant mines at the standard exit distance for a ship emerging from hyperspace near a planet. Then, while they're licking their wounds, we'll surround each ship one at a time, flying too close for the others to engage, and destroy them one by one."

"You think you can do that with the ships I am leaving you?" Sam questioned as he examined a rare painting.

"They'll never know what hit them."

"I suggest you also send out boarding craft and take over at least one of the enemy ships, then turn it against the others. The added firepower will help you and their confusion will hurt them."

"Makes sense. I'll keep it in mind," Pinal responded, his confident tone giving way to one of suspicion.

"Just make sure you succeed. It would be a shame for something to happen to that painting," Sam insinuated, then turned and left.

Merchanta
Revenue Central
Thursday, February 20th, 2708
6:00 P.M.

"All military operations within these territories are complete. I now relinquish all control to you, Governor Swanzia," Primary Canza stated for the benefit of the cameras.

"Thank you for your service, Primary Canza. I accept full governorship at this time," the governor responded as he shook Canza's hand. He then turned to address the cameras while Canza slipped out.

The governor was an Ordonian by birth, and had received the appointment because the emperor didn't trust a Merchant to run things in his name. However, as a reward for choosing to surrender at the end, the chairman was appointed adjutant governor, and now stood at Swanzia's side as he outlined his plans to the reporters. Standing against the wall behind them was Knight Captain Bazaine who continued in his role as royal observer.

"Are the pirates next, sir?" Farra asked, falling into step beside him.

"They are your next mission, yes. I'm headed back to Vehla. Take what ships you need and make sure they don't bother us again."

"Yes, sir!" Farra responded with a salute before rushing off.

He would eliminate the greed and corruption represented by the pirates while Canza saw to it the Vehlan territories continued their ascension to full imperial status. Their march to destiny continued, and would not be stopped.

Chapter Eighteen
Why We Fight

Swarnlia
Friday, February 21st, 2708
6:29 P.M.

We've been hiding for nearly two months, and the major still doesn't think we're ready to return to the fight! Helen Dodge stewed as she walked through town.

Since Major Briese had ordered that none of them go out alone, Private Exodus was with her, struggling to keep up as she stomped along in her rage.

"There's nothing we can do. Why can't you just accept that?" he managed to ask between breaths.

She ignored him.

If the rest of the team felt the same as him, then maybe it was time for her to strike out on her own. They might be able to give up and live with it, but she never could.

"Our destiny awaits!"

"None can stand in our way!"

The shouts cut through the storm raging inside her, and she traced the source to a pair of uniformed Ordonian soldiers walking down the opposite sidewalk. There was a platoon stationed in town to police the sector, and it appeared these two had just gotten off duty.

"The Vehlans couldn't even defend themselves. What made them think they could defend the interest?"

"Our strength is without equal. We've taught them that lesson twice now, and will teach it to them again if necessary."

"Why don't you shut up!" Exodus shouted from where he had stopped to catch his breath. Helen was far enough ahead of him so as to appear not to be with him, so she backed into the shadows of a nearby building to watch what happened.

Imperial soldiers weren't allowed to consume any alcohol, but these two were still drunk from their recent victories, so they quickly crossed the street and got in Exodus' face.

"Do you have something to say?"

"Yeah. If you're so strong, why did it take you a hundred years to defeat the union?"

"What would you know about strength?"

"I know you're avoiding my question."

"Fools like you really shouldn't speak."

"I think you're afraid to admit that the union was just as strong as you because that means you'll also be defeated one day," Exodus challenged, earning himself a punch to the gut.

"You have learned nothing. I suppose we'll have to give you a personal lesson."

The soldiers moved in to continue their attack, but Helen inserted herself between them and the private and held her hands in front of her apologetically.

"I'm sorry, Officers. My cousin never did learn when to keep his mouth shut. I'll take him home now."

"I can take them!" Exodus shouted, then tried to push past her, but she shoved him back with one arm.

"Now he's threatened us. We can't let that pass."

"Please, be patient. Both of his parents died in the war, and he hasn't gotten past it. He'll be fine once I get him home."

"If you do not step aside, we'll arrest both of you."

She didn't budge.

"Have it your way then."

Both of them tried to grab an arm, but she deftly spun to the right, shoving back the charging Exodus with just her left arm at the same time. The push was a little harder than she intended and the private fell to his butt on the hard sidewalk.

"What are you doing!" Exodus protested.

The soldiers didn't press the attack, apparently surprised by her display of agility and strength.

"All I wanted to do was take a walk, and you had to cause trouble. Now shut up and let me handle this!" she shouted back at her companion.

By now the commotion had attracted the attention of some civilians, but there weren't any other soldiers in sight.

"Fine, be on your way. Don't let us catch either of you making trouble again."

"Thank you, sir," Helen responded, then dragged Exodus to his feet and pulled him along with her. He finally had the good sense to stay quiet, but it was too little too late.

Dodge Family Farm
7:01 P.M.

"Inside!" Captain Dodge commanded as she shoved Exodus into the barn. The animals were out in the field, but they found Major Briese exercising in the center of the main room. He stopped when he saw them.

"What's going on?"

"He decided it would be a good idea to get into a fight with a couple Imp soldiers," she explained as she glared at Exodus.

"What is your problem? Aren't you the one that wants to fight?"

"Aren't you the one that wants to give up? You said as much seconds before getting mouthy with those soldiers."

"Yeah, but then I heard them talking and it made me mad. I thought you'd have my back."

"You're alive, aren't you?"

"Only because you begged them to let us go. Why didn't you fight them?"

"Because no matter what I want, I'm not going to put the team at risk!"

"What are you talking about?"

"She's saying that by getting into a fight with soldiers, you made them suspicious. It isn't hard for one soldier to recognize another, in or out of uniform, especially if they fight. When they report in, there will be an investigation," Breise explained.

"It wasn't that big a deal. I doubt they'll report it," Exodus responded.

"Ordonians report everything."

"I intervened before too much happened, but they were determined to teach him a lesson. It was only after I evaded their attack that they let us go," Helen reported.

"They gave up after you dodged a single attack?"

"That's right," Helen confirmed, and the major let out a resigned sigh.

"Then they must have realized you're an Azul Guardian."

"How could they possibly know that?" Exodus questioned.

"Either they've encountered one before, or more likely they've seen Star Knights in action. Such moves are not easily forgotten. We need to get out of here," Breise answered.

"Or you could turn yourselves in," a new voice suggested. They turned towards the main door to see that it was Helen's father.

"They'd kill us," Scopes stated from behind him, then he and Muddie stepped around him to join the rest of the team in the center of the room.

"The empire has offered amnesty to all union soldiers who give themselves up," Reuben responded.

"You can't possibly believe that!" Helen disputed.

"I do believe it. They released all their prisoners of war, and some who have turned themselves in have already returned to civilian life, and others are now serving as imperial soldiers. Clearly they mean what they say."

"The Imps never tell the whole truth. They may have released some, but there can be no doubt that there are others still in their custody."

"It's possible that they are giving amnesty to regular soldiers, but we are Azul Guardians. We're too dangerous, and they will see our executions as their only option," Briese expanded.

"You can earn their trust by cooperating with them."

That comment caused Helen to snort at his stupidity, but the major continued trying to reason with him.

"We also have to consider who else is in danger. The invasion of the Merchant's Interest shows they intend to continue their campaigns, and we can't just sit by while everyone is in danger."

The captain glanced at him in surprise, then quickly looked away to conceal her reaction.

So he hadn't given up on the fight after all.

"The Merchant's Interest was directly connected to the union and was harboring what remained of its military. It was only logical for the empire to attack."

"How can you not understand there is more to it than that!" Helen shouted. Her father glanced at her with complete calm, then looked at the rest of the team.

"Chancellor Macey officially dissolved the military when he surrendered. You don't have to follow orders from these two anymore, and can save yourselves."

Scopes and Muddie glanced at each other, then nodded a silent agreement before looking back at Reuben.

"I cannot justify saving myself while I know people are in danger. Someone has to stop the empire's genocide," Muddie stated.

"I saw a lot of bullies growing up on the streets, and have never much cared for them," Scopes added.

The last to decide, Exodus kept looking from the team to Reuben as they stared at him and awaited his response.

"I wanted out a year ago when they invaded Swarnlia, but stayed with you guys because I thought I had no other choice. Now I do."

"No one will think less of you if you want to leave," Breise assured him.

Helen would, but she chose not to voice this fact.

"Except that everything you're saying sounds right. The empire has to be stopped, and I'll never forgive myself if I quit now. I'll stay with you."

"You are throwing your lives away for nothing," Reuben challenged.

"That's what you've never understood. We don't fight for nothing; we fight for what we believe. All you care about is what happens in your own little world. Everything else can burn, so long as you are safe," Helen retorted.

Her father's only response was to shake his head and walk away.

A sadness so deep as to nearly overwhelm her swelled inside Helen as she watched him walk away, and she clenched her jaw to keep from showing it to the others.

This proved there would never be reconciliation between her and her family. They were forever strangers.

Chapter Nineteen
Imperial Triumph

OES Thunderstrike
Saturday, February 22nd, 2708
11:08 A.M.

Severe turbulence rocked the ship and seat restraints automatically activated, the fibers of Captain's Zenzal's uniform bonding with the chair to keep him securely seated.

"What happened?" he asked as the ship steadied.

"We exited hyperspace in the middle of a minefield, sir! We caught the shockwave from the vanguard exploding! All ten cruisers are destroyed!"

The captain cursed and slammed a fist on the arm of his chair. He should have predicted something like this.

"What's our status?"

"Minor burn damage to the outer hull. All systems operating at full capacity, sir," Tactical responded.

"Secondary Farra has ordered a cruiser group to clear the remaining mines, sir," Communications reported.

"Time?"

"Less than a minute, sir."

"Tactical display on main screen."

He frowned as he studied the readout where he could see only three gunships and a handful of assault fighters. The pirates had far more resources than that, so where were the rest of them?

"Secondary Farra has ordered us to move in and destroy the defenders, sir. Stormwind will cover us from behind."

"Tell him it's a trap and we need to send out scouts."

There was a short delay as the message was relayed to the secondary's ship, then the response came back asking how he knew that.

"The pirates have a lot more ships than we're seeing on our screens, and they must have had advance warning we were on our way. They're hiding somewhere, preparing to ambush us."

Another delay.

"Request denied, sir. He says to proceed as ordered."

Zenzal cursed the man's idiocy under his breath, but gave the order to proceed.

The pirates came at them, firing with everything they had, but they were no match for a dreadnaught. Their shields deflected the shots as if they were toys while their own weapons quickly dispatched the three gunships.

The fighter pilots proved to be highly skilled and managed to stay ahead of the Ordonian fighters and the ship's point defenses, but they could do no damage and they would be destroyed soon enough.

Then the ship shook from a series of hits and static clouded all the sensor displays.

"A large number of enemy reinforcements just dropped out of hyperspace, sir! We're getting hit on all sides!" Tactical reported, but the captain remained calm. He leaned over, placed one hand flat on the floor, and felt the vibrations from the hits.

"Stormwind is asking if we require assistance, sir," Communications relayed, but he ignored them.

"We're in no danger. There are more of them now, but we have time before they can do any real damage," he concluded for all to hear, then leaned back in his chair.

"We can't see them, sir, so how are we going to stop them?" his second-in-command asked.

"Network with the Stormwind and use their sensors to mark the targets. Fire when ready."

The screens cleared up seconds later to reveal thirty pirate vessels attacking them, a mix of gunships and fighters. Still less than he was expecting.

They returned fire, destroying over twenty of them in the first volley. The rest retreated into hyperspace, their ambush clearly having failed.

With the way clear, Secondary Farra took the lead and brought them into bombardment positions above the planet. They didn't have enough ships to cover the entire planet, but it wasn't necessary.

Several explosions rippled through the Thunderstrike, and emergency doors slammed shut in response to the computer detecting multiple hull breaches.

"Boarders!"

"So that's their game. They intend to take our ship and turn it against the rest of the fleet," Zenzal said to no one in particular. At least their plan made sense now.

The pirates knew they could never defend against an Ordonian fleet, so they had chosen to use only what resources they needed to take one of the attacking ships for themselves. They blinded their sensors long enough to get their boarding craft in place, obviously hoping to take them by surprise.

"How many of them are there?"

"I can see ten boarding craft, each one with a capacity of twenty-five, sir."

"Two-hundred fifty? Don't they know we have over two-thousand marines on this ship, not to mention the gun emplacements?" the second-in-command wondered aloud.

"Security footage on the main screen," Zenzal ordered, and the tactical display was replaced with ten video frames showing where the pirates had entered.

Most of them showed marines checking fallen pirates to make sure they were dead, while a few showed prisoners being corralled. Only one showed any fighting, and it was only because the pirates had managed to take cover in a storage room with only one entrance. They wouldn't last much longer.

"Secondary Farra has fired on the planet, sir."

"Show me."

The tactical screen reappeared to show a nuclear missile streaking towards what appeared to be the biggest pirate base. Both missile and base disappeared from the screen minutes later.

"This is Secondary Farra of the Ordeon Empire to all pirates remaining on the planet's surface. Your defense has failed, and we have destroyed your central command. Surrender, or die."

They received the surrender signal within seconds, and troops were sent down to secure the remaining bases.

As the ground teams reported in, Zenzal couldn't shake the feeling that it was all too easy and there still weren't as many pirates here as there should be, but he finally decided the rest must be out on raids or occupying bases on other planets. Now that their main base of operations was gone, they would no longer be a problem.

Vehla
2:13 P.M.

"Good work, Farra. Prepare interrogations for the prisoners to see if they know anything we can use, then assign someone else to oversee the rest of the process," Canza responded to his secondary's report of victory at Altaius, then cut the connection.

He watched through the cockpit window as his shuttle approached the space station, one of two he had ordered constructed upon taking command of the invasion force over a year ago. They'd appropriated a couple of orbital docks the Vehlans had used for their space races, then retrofitted them to his purposes.

The shuttle docked, and he disembarked into a security station where he patiently allowed the guards to verify his identity using DNA scans. When they were finished, he entered an elevator and told it to take him to an observation deck.

This was an idea he had been working on for many years, but hadn't been able to put into action until recently. Now these orbital shipyards worked around the clock to make his dream a reality.

To maintain secrecy, he hired eligible Vehlans from the planet below and gave them living quarters aboard the station. Not even the emperor knew about this yet, and he wanted to keep it that way.

He had been fully prepared to turn everything over to whomever Lentaise assigned as planetary governor, but was only too happy to keep it to himself when he turned out to be that person.

The lift finally reached its destination, and the doors opened out to a circular room with a single, transparent wall. He stepped up to the wall, and peered down at the ship frame below him. One couldn't tell much about it at the moment, except that it was big, even bigger than a dreadnaught.

It was to be the first of a new class of ship, the most powerful ship ever constructed by mankind.

Nothing will stop us.

If you enjoyed *Triumphant Empire,* continue the story in *Revolution!*

Appendix A
Characters

Leon Tyquese (Colonel)

Age: 37
Gender: Male
Ethnicity: Vehlan
Hair Color/Style: Brown/Military Cut
Eye Color: Grey
Height: 5', 7"
Build: Lean, Athletic

Leon was born on the planet Vehla, homeworld of a nation that had been at war for over seventy years. As soon as he was old enough to understand, he embraced the patriotism of his people and dedicated his life to their cause.

He joined the Vehlan Union infantry as a commissioned officer once he was of age, and served with excellence, his stubborn resolve inspiring those around him to fight harder while his insightful tactics often turned certain defeat into victory. This pattern of service eventually earned him a promotion to the staff of General Reno, commander-in-chief of the union military.

Military service was still voluntary at this time, but preparation programs for children were prevalent with the expectation that nearly everyone would end up choosing to serve.

As long as he remains alive, Leon Tyquese will continue to fight tyranny no matter the odds.

Sam Tyquese (Captain)

Pirate Designation: Red Sam
Age: 34
Gender: Male
Ethnicity: Vehlan
Hair Color/Style: Black/Short
Eye Color: Grey
Height: 5', 6"
Build: Thick, Muscular

The world that Sam was born into was one that had been at war for nearly eighty years. Despite the zealous patriotism that permeated his culture, he never wanted anything to do with that war and wished only to live his own life doing what he loved. This didn't sit well with his parents or older brother Leon, the latter of which constantly pressured him into attending the military preparation programs for children.

When it came time to enlist, he reluctantly joined the Vehlan Union fleet. His performance was average in that he properly performed any task assigned to him, but he never did anything more than was required of him.

A confrontation with a superior officer led to his desertion in no longer caring what anyone else thought. Now a fugitive with no place to go, he made his way to the pirate planet where he joined the red faction.

In fighting to survive, he learned how to thrive.

Max Canza (Primary)

Age: 39
Gender: Male
Ethnicity: Ordonian
Hair Color/Style: Bronze/Military Cut
Eye Color: Dark Blue
Height: 6', 3"
Build: Medium, Athletic

As the only child of moderately wealthy parents in the Ordeon Empire, Max was raised to be their greatest achievement in life. They enrolled him in advanced schooling and physical training with the requirement he excel at every task given to him. He embraced this life, managing to exceed everyone's expectations and even seeking out new challenges on his own.

Since he was committed to a lifelong military career, Max chose to complete his education before joining. His pattern of excellence continued in both school and as a military officer. When he successfully completed a seemingly impossible mission, he came to the attention of the emperor himself who then assigned him command of the final invasion of their enemy's homeworld.

Now Max is right where he needs to be to finally crush his people's worst enemy and open the way to achieving their destiny.

Helen Dodge (Captain)

Nickname: Dodger
Age: 31
Gender: Female
Ethnicity: Swarnlian (Vehlan Province)
Hair Color/Style: Dark Red/Military Cut
Eye Color: Dark Green
Height: 5', 9"
Build: Medium, Athletic

A rebel from the moment she was born, Helen has always clashed with the people around her, including her own family with her mother being the only one to show any real patience with her. As a child she would often go off alone into town or the woods around her home to explore, further developing her independent personality and learning self-reliance.

A strong desire to stand with her people against the Ordeon Empire did nothing to curb her rebellious nature and new conflicts arose after joining the officer's academy. This is until Peter Briese, a visiting special forces operative, saw something in her and got her transferred to Azul Guardian training.

Upon successful completion of the course, she returned to the academy and finished her schooling, after which her mentor added her to his team. Her companions know not to get on her bad side, but they also recognize no one is more loyal or better to have with them in a fight.

Appendix B Factions

Main Factions

Ordeon Empire

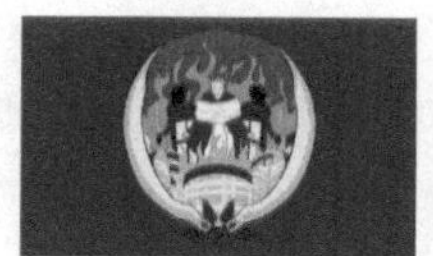

Type of Government: Imperial Monarchy
Head of State: Emperor
Economy: Imperialist/Capitalist
Homeworld: Ordeos
Capital City: Ordeos Prime
Controlled Systems: 21 Provinces

The Ordeon Empire has been on a quest of total domination since its inception, held in check only by the Vehlan Union. Their reasons for this quest have varied throughout history, but presently imperial citizens honestly believe the empire is humanity's only hope for a brighter future. If others refuse to acknowledge this fact, then they are holding the human race back and must be eliminated.

At least six years of military service is required of all citizens. The youngest age they can join is eighteen, but they are given the choice of joining right away or completing their schooling before joining. This system ensures the empire's military maintains the maximum possible strength at all times.

Vehlan Union (Destroyed)

Type of Government: Democratic Republic
Head of State: Chancellor
Economy: Capitalist
Homeworld: Vehla
Capital City: United
Controlled Systems: 17

Originally formed out of several nations for the purpose of mutual defense and easier trade, the Vehlan Union was originally intended to remain a group of sovereign nations working together, but eventually became a single nation.

The nation has always sought to maintain individual liberty for all people, even non-citizens, which resulted in them fighting several wars with the Ordeon Empire to halt its campaigns of conquest.

Military service was optional until the last few years of the Hundred Years War, but strong patriotism moved most citizens to join despite not being required to do so.

Pirate League

Type of Government: Confederate
Head of State: Red Captain
Economy: Criminal
Homeworld: Altaius
Capital City: N/A
Controlled Systems: 1

The six pirate factions historically cooperated with one another only as necessary for survival, but that changed when the remnants of the Vehlan military joined with Red Sam and helped him to defeat his rival. This made the red faction powerful enough to take over all the others by force which led to Sam demanding they submit to his authority. They agreed and formed themselves into the Pirate League under his command.

Most of the pirates were actually deserters from either the Vehlan or Ordonian militaries who had grown disillusioned with the war and were left with no other choice but a life of crime. They didn't know it at first, but the league was formed to be a resistance movement against the Ordeon Empire. When Red Sam and his brother Leon finally told them the truth, they were able to convince them to be willing participants in exchange for amnesty and the promise of a normal life.

Appendix C Glossary of Terms

Ship Tags

(The acronym before a ship's name designating its affiliation.)

G.C.S. - Galactic Confederacy Ship
O.E.S. - Ordeon Empire Ship
R.P.S. - Red Pirate Ship
V.U.S. - Vehlan Union Ship

Bridge Stations

In the interest of saving time, the operator of each bridge station is referred to by the name of that station as if it were their own name. This way a commanding officer only has to call out for the station he/she wants, and not for the person operating the station at that particular moment. Stations on larger ships are operated by more than one officer, so the senior officer is the one who will respond to orders or requests for information.

On smaller ships, some of these stations are combined, but following is a list of each one as a separate entity.

Helm - The pilot's station responsible for the flight operations of the craft. Normally crewed by a single operator.

Navigation - This station controls the sensors which monitor navigational hazards around the ship such as asteroids and gravity wells and also contains detailed charts for plotting courses through hyperspace. It is usually crewed by one or two operators or is combined with the helm station.

Tactical - The position overseeing a vessel's combat systems including threat detection and targeting sensors, shield operation, and weapons. Normally crewed by one personnel but can have up to five, with the additional officers adding the ability to monitor other ships in a formation.

Systems - This station is responsible for overseeing all ship functions which do not fall under a specialized category, such as life support and cargo/personnel transfers. Operated by between three to seven crew.

Communications - The station responsible for all internal and external communications aboard ship. Up to four personnel can be assigned here, but on smaller ships it is combined with the tactical station.

Threat Conditions

Each national military operates under a common set of threat conditions. It's believed that this system was put in place when the human race was unified under one banner, but there is no evidence to support this fact.

Condition Yellow - No threat detected. Shields at minimum. Weapons deactivated. Crew maintains alertness, watching at all times for any possible threats. Standard operating condition for every military vessel.

Condition Orange - Possible threat detected. Shields at maximum. Weapons placed in standby. On-duty crew called to battle stations.

Condition Red - Threat confirmed. Shields at maximum. Weapons activated. Fighters launched. All crew to battle stations. Power diverted to combat systems.

Damage Levels

When ships are damaged during the course of a battle, commanding officers need to instantly know the extent of the damage. Toward that end, a system is in place that conveys that information with one or two words.

Minor - Shields damaged. Possible damage to hull. No systems affected.

Moderate - Shields heavily damaged, possibly collapsed. Damage to the hull. Some systems are damaged and/or disabled.

Heavy - Shields off-line. Significant damage to hull, with possible breaches. Several systems are damaged, disabled, or destroyed. Ship is still battle capable.

Severe - All battle systems disabled or destroyed. Significant damage to hull. Ship may still be capable of flight, or is completely disabled.

Destroyed - The ship is damaged beyond hope of repair but parts and materials may still be salvageable.

Miscellaneous Terms

Imp - A slang term used by Vehlans to denote people of Ordonian origin. It is short for "Imperial," but is also a reference to the mythological creature as a way to say the empire and its citizens are evil.

Nihl - A slang term used by Ordonians for people from the Vehlan Union. It comes from the word "Nihilist" and is meant to say that Vehlans have no respect for law and order. A secondary meaning references the philosophical ideas about nothingness which is their way of saying the Vehlans are nothing compared to them.

Palco - Short for palm-computer, this is a microcomputer embedded in the palm of the hand which is accessed via a holographic interface activated by a specific muscle movement which is chosen by the user. It is also the name of the first commercial distributor of the product, but the term is now used in reference to all such devices regardless of the brand.

Acknowledgements

Thank you to my dad for his continued support and encouragement on this never-ending journey of mine.

Special thanks to artist Calley Dunnihoo who created the first cover and has stuck with me on this journey from the first edition to the current revision.

And to all my friends who tolerate my rambling on about non-existent worlds and my constant requests for feedback.

About the author

An active imagination has been one of Dodge's defining attributes for as long as he can remember, with its creations often seeming more real to him than the world in which he lived. Upon discovering a talent and affinity for the written word, he began writing stories for fun at first, then eventually decided to make it more than a hobby. This has taught him to control his wandering mind while also providing an escape for him and others.

Born in northern Illinois, his family moved to southern Missouri shortly afterward where he currently lives with his two cats Merry and Pippin who provide comfort and drive him crazy multiple times a day. He rides a motorcycle, exercises regularly, and trains in Brazilian Jiu-Jitsu when possible.

Also by Dodge Merrin

Follow me on Amazon!

Embers of Hope Science Fiction Miniseries

Triumphant Empire

Available through Amazon & KU.

Revolution

Available through Amazon.

Total War

Available through Amazon.

Brink of Extinction

Available through Amazon.

See Also

Humble Glory

Available through Amazon & KU.

www.ingramcontent.com/pod-product-compliance
Lightning Source LLC
LaVergne TN
LVHW090604110826
845146LV00001B/263

* 9 7 9 8 9 9 0 9 0 7 9 2 8 *